MW01139530

REGALI

To Mum, Grandma Joan, Nan Evelyn and Great-Nans Regina and Olga ... the wise women in my life

REGALI

Jaymin Eve

Regali

Copyright © Jaymin Eve 2014

All rights reserved

First published in 2014

Eve, Jaymin

Regali

1st edition

No part of this book may be reproduced, stored in a retrieval system or transmitted in any form or by any means, without the prior permission in writing of the publisher, nor be otherwise circulated in any form of binding or cover other than that in which it is published and without a similar condition, including this condition, being imposed on the subsequent purchaser. All characters in this publication other than those clearly in the public domain are fictitious, and any resemblance to real persons, living or dead, is purely coincidental.

Chapter 1

Ria

The two jag men waved their fronds, swishing around the tropical heat which encased Ria's loft house. They had insisted on this task, but in reality the humidity did not bother Ria; she had been born in the rainforest and her blood hummed within the confines of this damp and natural environment.

Rising from her day bed, Ria stretched to her full height, working out all of the kinks from her slumber. A few beads of sweat rolled along her body, usual for the weather here.

She waved off the jags. They gave a brief bow to their queen before departing and leaving her to the morning ritual. Clothed only in her tawny skin, Ria strode across to the large opening which was hung with threaded vines to separate her home in the tree tops from the rest of the jungle. With the barest of thoughts the barrier shifted out of her way. She thanked her beloved plants with a blown kiss.

Standing in the perfect still of the jungle, Ria absorbed the glow of the six moons surrounding Regali. They cast soft filtered light through the dense wilderness. Her platform was two miles high, in one of the older trees, allowing the most unrestricted view of her territory.

Ria thought of the tales from the south. She'd never left her home but she had heard that other countries had clear land and expanses of flat grass-plains. She couldn't really imagine that. Her country was the jungle of Artwon and there was no free space. They must feel exposed, not having the protection of undergrowth and high level tree tops.

"Ria!"

She was not startled by the growled greeting. Her best friend and bodyguard was Klea, a leon. She turned around. The blue-tinged light from the moons highlighted the female standing in her doorway. She was shorter than Ria, as were all in this jungle, except the bera pack. Klea's mane was a dark golden color, long down her back and wrapping around to coat her forehead and cheeks. The rest of her fur covering was a lighter gold, the same color as her eyes.

"You are well?" Klea said gruffly. Her vocal cords only resonated in a low rough sound.

Ria nodded. "For once I slept uninterrupted. The tree spirits kept the dreams away."

Klea growled. "The tree spirits? I do not know why you ask anything of them. They are your family and still you must be indebted to them after each favor."

Ria's mother, Theanine, was the matriarch of the tree spirits. The gods of Regali. Theanine was literally mother-to-nature. None of the spirits existed on the physical plane any longer. Ria was the last to walk with the beasts. Her mother had taken a temporary corporeal form to conceive and grow her child. But then she had returned to the spiritual plane.

"You know that there must be equilibrium; if I take I must also give. The spirits keep the natural balance." Ria was steadfast in her defense of her mother's people.

Right now Ria was the most powerful creature in Artwon. All living plants heeded and obeyed her call. And for this reason she was Queen of the beasts who lived within these jungles. There were six main packs. The jags: small cat people; leon: large cat people; bera: grizzlies; eaglet: the flyers; slimes: reptiles; and munks: the apes. The smaller or mixed breeds were scattered around, mostly keeping to themselves.

"Where am I visiting today?" Ria asked as she clothed herself in leather and vines.

The sparse two-piece set had been weaved from an array of donated skins from the packs. It was the right of the Queen to wear her people. In the long past the packs would sacrifice members for the honor of the leader wearing their skin. Today, thankfully, the leather was from those naturally fallen.

"It is the morning before the red moon, Ria. You must convene with the tree spirits and prepare for the shifting."

A smile spread across Ria's full lips. She should have known. Her blood was boiling this morning and her spirit extra restless. She was not pack and did not have to shift on the red moon, but she still felt the pull. Striding forward, her long mahogany hair fell almost to her calves. With her innate agility she leapt from the outer branch, landing in the next tree. From here she took a vine down to the ground level.

The thick undergrowth hugged her legs in greeting. A quick pause by the reflective pool where she bathed gave her time to trail a hand along her favorite purple calia flowers. Their iridescent color was a perfect match for her own eyes. Her mother surrounded this area with the beautiful but deadly flower, as she knew they soothed Ria's soul. The benefit of having a nature goddess as her mother. The negative was, of course, never having her physically around. Ria had been raised with the leons, hence why Klea was her best friend.

"Let's go, you have many miles to traverse this morning." Klea spoke after clawing her way down to where Ria stood.

They started at a run, in the direction of the sixth moon, toward the sacred tree. The undergrowth was dense, but that posed no problem. The plants and vines simply shifted for them. Ria had already sent out her energy along their path to let the forest know she needed a clear run. With the help of her plants they would be at their destination in no time.

She kneeled, allowing her chestnut-colored hair to fan around her; the vines that were imprinted across it shimmered green. Ria closed her eyes, her hands reaching forward to lie flat-palmed against the sacred one. It was the first tree in Regali's existence, and from where all the tree spirits were born. Ria felt her energy separate from her being and entwine with the warmth of her ancestors. Words were never spoken out loud or internally; it was simply a joining of spirit, a moment for thanks and recharge.

"Queen."

Her head snapped up at the interruption. No one was ever to disturb her during these blessed moments. Where was Klea? Suddenly her friend moved into view. She had her muscled arms locked around the throat of a munk.

"Sorry, Ria, I was too slow to cut off his vocal cord access." Klea lowered her head, shame spreading across her cat-like features.

Ria waved her hand, rising from her kneeling position to stand before them.

"Let him speak," she said.

Klea growled at these words.

"He would not have disturbed me if it wasn't important," Ria finished. She had great faith in her people. They were honorable.

With one last rumble from her chest, Klea loosened her muscular arms, allowing the munk to suck in a deep breath. His dark fur was disheveled, but it was more the panic in his eyes which moved Ria.

"Speak without fear," she told him, flicking her head at Klea so she would back up a few steps.

"I apologize, your most majestic one." He spoke in the tongue of the beasts, which had taken Ria many years to understand.

It was far different to the words of the gods that she spoke.

"I have been sent from my pack. We need your help. The fringe are back."

Ria straightened, adrenalin flooding her system. She winced as Klea's roar of pain and anger echoed throughout the jungle foliage. The fringe, as this group of misfits was known, had killed Klea's sister: Agia. Ria also mourned the loss of Agia. They had been searching for the fringe's hidden territory for years, but so far the plants were keeping it secret, even from Ria.

"How many of them?" she asked as they started to run.

"At least ten," he said.

There was no time to waste. The fringe had not been seen for many red moons, and this was a chance to stop the carnage. Ria mentally called for her people.

They had a system where the plants around each of the six packs' territories would alert them. Each pack had trained guards who had pledged their loyalty to her, but unlike other queens, she did not have them by her side all the time. She preferred they stayed to protect their packs, only leaving if she called for their help. But the fringe were strong and dangerous, made up of rogue members from every pack and, since they killed indiscriminately, Ria knew she would need help. Plus, each pack deserved the chance to avenge its dead.

They were fast through the jungle. Klea and the munk used the trees, flying through the higher canopy. Ria was safer on the ground, her plants lending their assistance. The heat continued to beat down, humidity coating her shining skin. The six moons that circled Regali kept their world warm, and when the red moon rose, the heat's intensity increased. Ria tried to calm herself as she travelled. As Queen she needed to keep the situation from escalating. She could never let go of her base instincts and unleash the fury inside. But these misfits were testing her patience as they wrought a path of destruction through the packs. She had to protect her people.

The munks' territory was in the south of Artwon, where the trees were extra high and the undergrowth sparse. Ria could hear calls echoing through the greenery. The soldiers of the packs were moving through the jungle, preparing to descend on the fringe.

Artwon wasn't a large country and the packs lived reasonably close to each other. There were many rules for co-habitating, and if they were broken by any members then there was a trial by their peer group and the final sentence was dealt with by the Queen.

It was these rules which had offended the animalistic sentimentality of the fringe members. They wanted to fight and war without repercussion. But Ria would be dead and back with her ancestors before she let anarchy rule the packs. Her appointment as Queen had been a hard-fought battle. For the first time in history Artwon was ruled by someone not of the packs. She had worked to tame them, although it was wise to never forget their animal sides.

With a brief mental command Ria lifted her arms and called for the vines she used to swing herself through the trees. She was fast and had unlimited stamina, but that was nothing compared to that of the packs, and so this was the easiest way for her to keep up with them.

To her left five slimes swung into view. They nodded their heads in a deferential greeting to her. On her right were the jags. She could see bera grizzly guards beneath her, thrashing through the undergrowth. She winced as her plants were trampled. Her energy cleared the rest of the path, saving any further plant deaths.

The vines continued to swing her in graceful arcs. Her advanced hearing detected the echoes of screams from the munks' territory. She urged her journey on faster. She needed to get there now; the fringe members were probably tearing them apart. As a rule the munks were smart, agile and quick, but in brute strength they were near the bottom of the packs, except for their ape guards. But by the sounds of it they were in trouble.

The vines propelled her through the outer perimeter of the munks' territory.

And suddenly the carnage came into view.

The mangled body of a female munk, crouched over her two babies, was the first thing Ria saw. Pain exploded in Ria's chest and she let out a cursing shriek that rang through the trees.

She had been too late for that family.

The plants around her immediately reacted to her pain and anger. The jungle sprang to life: vines shooting around, branches descending and being used as weapons by the pack guards.

Ria's rapid observations determined that the messenger munk had been mistaken. There were not ten; there were at least three dozen fringe members. They were easy to discern by the red streaked throughout their fur. This was their gory calling card: blood of the enemies. And they were organized. Half of them were fighting through the pack, keeping them all occupied, whilst the other half were stealing food and healing stores.

"No!"

The messenger munk was crouched over the fallen body of the female and young. He had gathered them into his arms, rocking back and forward, his howls ringing through the screams and fighting.

Ria's heart ached for him. But before she could move closer, a tiny cry could be heard. The munk's head flew up in shock and Ria couldn't believe what she was seeing.

One of the babies crawled out from under its mother and into his arms. Followed by the second baby. Ria felt both relieved and saddened; their mother had died protecting them, but at least they had not been sacrificed.

The munk cradled both the tiny creatures in his arms. As he stood he caught Ria's eye.

She could see his need for help and sent the vines to him. They formed a safe netting into which he reluctantly released his offspring. As Ria's warm energy mingled with the plants, she asked the vines to take and protect the young until she called for them. The greenery disappeared up into the canopy.

The munk dropped beside his mate again, kissing her once on the head and closing her eyes before he stood and turned away.

Ria lost him as he plunged into the crowd. The other packs' guards had arrived now and they soon had the fringe members surrounded.

As Ria strode over to the main group she wondered why they'd allowed themselves to be caught. Fringe did not usually come in willingly.

A burst of noise had her spinning around and a vine snatched her up just as another large group of beras flooded the munks' territory.

Their fur was speckled with blood.

From her secure position, Ria was able to send the rest of the vines to seize her people, saving them from the ferocity of the new arrivals' attacks. Beras stood over ten feet tall, strong and brutal with razor claws and jaws full of massive teeth. For some reason more of this pack had defected to the fringe than any other.

After rescuing their members, the fringe disappeared into the jungle, taking with them the munks' supplies.

Ria followed using the sight of her plants, hoping to be led to their territory. The plants were her best chance of keeping up with the fringe. The guards were in pursuit but were already a step behind.

And then midway through Artwon, as they neared the old waterfall, the fringe members simply disappeared. It was always the same, and she couldn't understand how they hid from the jungle. She searched aimlessly for a few more minutes, but the foliage sensed no disturbance at all.

Pulling her energy from the trees she focused back on the scene in the munks' territory. The vines dropped her down and she rushed to offer help and comfort. The screams of grief were deafening as packs found loved ones dead.

Ria joined with those moving to tend to the injured. She spent many hours using her knowledge of healing and plants to fix wounds, poisons and breaks. Finally, as the moons shifted higher in the sky, they began to bury the dead and rest the injured.

Ria called for the vines with the two babies. She had been keeping an eye on them and they had slept through most of the pandemonium. Reaching out, she gently captured the sleeping munks, their sweet little faces so peaceful. She looked around for the father, but he was nowhere to be seen. Finally, as she wandered away from the main gathering, she found him. He had been missed when they tended to the injured.

He was curled up beside his mate, one of his hands resting on hers, the other pressed tightly to the wound in his chest.

Ria's breath caught in her throat.

The munk's chest rose and fell very lightly, but she could see the torn damage to his chest was too much for a recovery. Tears pricked at the corner of her eyes. She glanced down at the innocence in her arms, tiny little faces with brown fur so soft and silky. They were too young to remember their parents, to realize their entire worlds had been ripped apart.

"Ria, why do you hold these young?" Klea, who had been her shadow for most of the battle, spoke from behind her.

"Their parents were killed." She pointed toward the fallen couple, and as she spoke the male took his last breath, his body relaxing into the stillness of death.

She shed a few more tears, her life water falling into the soil.

"Let us finish helping their recovery and then we will return to the sacred tree," Ria said, turning away from the heart-wrenching scene.

She needed to speak with the tree spirits about the fringe. This had to stop now. Their ferocity was increasing, the carnage heartbreaking. It was Ria's job to save her people, but she was making no inroads into stopping them. She just couldn't understand why her plants hid these extremists from her.

"Queen." A female munk stepped in front of her. "I am Aralet, sister to Ara." She pointed to the still body of the little ones' father. "I will take the children and raise them."

She spoke bluntly but with respect. Ria knew that even if Ara had no blood relatives, someone from the pack would have cared for these two young. At that moment the elder of the two children held out its arms to Aralet, and Ria could see they knew each other. Leaning down, she laid a gentle kiss on top of their heads before she passed them across to their brethren.

"Care for them well," she said, before turning to follow Klea.

They had many more hours work helping to salvage and rebuild the munks' territory. All of which had to be done before the red moon.

Ria was silent in her loft house, watching, waiting for the full crest of the red moon. The six smaller moons cast their shade of blue, but as the large red circle rose above the canopy, the world turned to purple. And at the peak of the red moon howls rang free. Ria threw back her head, savoring the spill of energy through her blood. It was rare that she ventured down to run with the packs. This was their time to be free and not feel their Queen was watching over their shoulders. But sometimes she wished to be pack. To lose all forms of civilized behavior for a short time.

"I have to go now." Klea's rough tone startled Ria.

She spun around to find the leon in mid transition. The skin was melting away to be replaced by fur and when Klea's mouth finally lengthened into a muzzle she would no longer be able to speak in human tongue.

Ria nodded. She knew Klea hated leaving her unguarded, but no pack member could ignore the call of the red moon. And she would be safe.

With a roar, Klea dropped to all fours and flung herself out of the doorway. Ria moved back to the edge of the trees, watching as her jungle came to life. The noise below was almost deafening.

Ria never slept the night of the red moon. The energy had her buzzing around her loft until the purple light faded and the large ball disappeared from the sky. The moment that the blue moons filled the sky, the packs quietened and proceeded to sleep off the night. Ria took advantage of this time, descending to the forest floor and moving freely through Artwon. She needed this moment to release her overload of energy. Each time power fizzling from her plants sprouted or burst to life. Large flowers bloomed, fruit blossomed, and she loved feeding her overflow back into nature.

During her run she'd never seen any living creatures, so an unexpected movement between two lanta trees had her grinding to a halt.

Pack members required at least twelve hours' sleep after the red moon, so it could be none of them. Ria scanned the dense vines and trees as she wandered under the large brown trunks that formed the structure for the tangled venus vines.

There was no more movement, but she knew something had disturbed the land; she could feel the unease from the plants.

Deciding that whatever it was must be long gone, she was turning to continue her journey when he stepped out from between a section of large vines.

Ria gasped.

She knew this man.

Her mother had given her dreams of the father she'd never known. The father who was now standing before her.

She took an involuntary step forward, her eyes cataloguing every detail. He was much taller than she was, his hair the same silky brown color as her own, his skin much darker but still tawny. Ria had always known that her unusual eye color was from him, but his were even more dramatically set off by stunning purple square-shaped marks running along the right side of his face and neck.

Except for these marks, she was the female version of this man. Well, the marks and the ivy print in her hair, which was courtesy of her mother.

They examined each other. Ria could see the vines curling around his arms and legs, the same way they did when greeting her. And then as she continued to stare at him the marks disappeared off his face, as if they'd just melted into his skin. How had he done that?

"You are very impressive." He finally spoke, his accent heavy and unfamiliar.

"What are you doing here?" Ria asked him.

"I have watched you for a long time. Your mother asked that I leave you alone." His purple eyes flashed, reflecting off the blue moonlights. "But things are changing in the First World star system. It's no longer safe, so I'm here to warn you."

Ria's unease grew, which had her plants wrapping tightly around her for comfort.

"Warn me about what?" she asked.

He held out a hand to her. "It would be better if I showed you."

Ria hesitated. She knew nothing of him or his intentions. But despite this she found herself stepping forward and reaching out to place her smaller hand into his.

"Show me the threat to my people."

Ria stared at the bunkers under the roots of the massive rairing tree, energy roaring inside her. She had the barest sliver of control over her anger.

Her father, whose name she had learnt was Nos, had shown her how the fringe had been evading her detection.

They wore the skins of the dead.

That was why when she scanned the forest for them they went undetected: the skin of all those they had killed surrounded their den like a large camouflage, and they also covered themselves in the skins. The deads' fur gave off its own aura, hiding the living who wore it. And they had hundreds of furs, many more dead than she'd ever realized.

"As terrible as you may find this, I did not bring you here to mourn your dead." Nos spoke quietly. "These nuisances are the gateway to something much worse that could spell the end of Artwon and Regali."

He definitely had Ria's attention now. She waited for him to continue, but he seemed content to sit beside her in the high branches. Patience was a skill she'd worked hard to develop in her many years, so for now she just continued to observe.

The fringe had numerous members. Hundreds came and went through the veil of dead.

Ria sat upright, her senses firing as a group emerged from the underground burrow. They weren't pack. They looked like her, but short and sturdy, the dwarvin. She had heard of these creatures. They lived in the lands of the north; the flat plains.

"What are they doing here?" she muttered.

"War is coming to your doorstep, Ria. The fringe are gathering rebel factions from all corners of Regali. They plan on taking Artwon first."

His words sent shockwaves of panic through her. There had never been war between the countries before. As a rule, everyone stuck to their own area.

"They could not have organized this on their own," she said, knowing the fringe did not have the manpower or the resources.

The north men disappeared into the trees. She was tempted to send out her vines and steal back her dead brethren they wore, but she knew now wasn't the time to tip them off.

"That is why I have come," Nos said. "You have a Walker problem."

Chapter 2

Abigail

Six days.

We'd been stuck inside the moonstale dome for six days, and in this time it was abundantly clear that while Walkers were powerful they were mostly – what was the right word? – oh yeah, asshats.

Most of them had no clue how the modern world worked and they threw their dominance around like bullying children in the playground. And, speaking of children, I'd finally asked about Walker young.

There were none at this gathering. Brace said their rare offspring were protected and would never be involved in mass Walker events. I had a strange longing to see the power, majesty and beauty of Walker children. Something told me they would be mesmerizing.

The last six days of the gathering had been a power play amongst the clans. It was so frustrating. Everyone knew that the older clan members held more information than could ever be recorded. And if we could get them to stop hoarding their thoughts we might have some clues to defeating the Seventine. Easier said than done. I was starting to worry that the entire gathering was a fruitless endeavor.

Right at that moment I was hiding away in the trees by the lake. Some of the very old Doreen members were scattered close by, but unlike their newer models, they mostly left me alone. I was sitting in the forest worrying about everything. The clans, the Seventine and lastly Lucy.

Something was going on with her; she was keeping a secret from me, which was very unlike her. I was worried that it might have something to do with Colton. He'd been sniffing around my best friend like the wolf he was, and I was contemplating a way to neuter him.

I'll be finished soon, Red. Then I'm coming for you.

I shivered as the deep tones of my mate brushed across my mind. It had been a long six days for Brace also. His father's death had left his Walker clan, Abernath, in a state of disarray. Brace was now on the verge of becoming Abernath's next Princep, and I wasn't sure how I felt about this. He wasn't even the ruler yet and I'd barely seen him over the past week. I missed him.

Promises, promises, I teased him. *What if you can't find me?*

He laughed.

You're in a moonstale dome that you can't escape. I don't think that will be a problem.

The Walker gathering was scheduled to last for seven days and in that time no one could leave this area. It had made for some interesting fights and challenges, but so far nothing too major had happened. But that might all change tonight. This was the final meeting and all the Princeps had agreed to reveal their collected information about the Seventine. So far they had been less than forthcoming, no one wanting to just give their knowledge away for free.

I was hoping that we would discover something which could be used to swing the battle-of-the-star-systems in our favor. Right now we had too little time and information and we were running against the clock. I had to finish gathering the seven half-Walker girls before the Seventine were all released. Right now I had Talina from Spurn and Fury from Crais. And tomorrow I was off to

Regali, the planet of the beasts. Meanwhile the three freed Seventine were around severing tethers and exploding Walkers. Luckily for us, we hadn't seen any evidence that the third had stuck around after killing Que.

"Abbs, I need to tell you something."

I spun around at the sound of my best friend's somber tone. One look at her face had panic zooming through my veins. I'd known she was keeping something from me but this was bad, really bad.

"Oh, my god, Luce, what the hell happened?"

She opened her mouth but I kind of lost my mind as the worst case scenario I could imagine jumped into my thoughts. Damn Colton.

"You're pregnant, aren't you? Shit. I'm going to kill that mangy flea bag."

I knew what I was saying was crazy, but I couldn't stop myself turning away and marching into the Doreens' area. The horror spreading across Lucy's face only increased my panic.

"Colton," I bellowed as I strode from the forest and into Doreen. He was somewhere with Brace. "Get your hairy butt out here."

"Abby!" Lucy was at my side. "What the crap are you doing? I'm not pregn –"

"Are you looking for me?" Colton strolled over, his perfect face relaxed.

"You have some explaining to do, rug man," I said, my annoyance fueling my words.

I'd warned Lucy to stay away from this Walker, but clearly she hadn't listened.

"Rug man?" he asked, raising his brows.

"Yeah, because you're about a minute from becoming a pelt on my floor," I spat out. "What did you do? Lucy has been keeping a secret from me and there's only one thing that would freak her out that much."

His white blue eyes flicked across to lock on Lucy's face.

"She thinks I'm having a litter," Lucy said, raising her brows.

I couldn't even think how this had happened. I mean, I knew *how* it happened, but it wasn't that simple with a Walker. Half-Walkers aren't supposed to exist, except the seven of us who were needed to save the worlds, but I couldn't think of any other reason why Lucy had been avoiding me for days. And I knew it was early, she wasn't showing or anything, but I assumed she'd found out in a vision.

Colton's features hardened. "Why does she think that?" His tone was deadly calm. "Have you been doing something to get pregnant? Who?" He threw his hands in the air. "I'll kill him."

Shit, sounds like it's not Colton's.

25

Lucy narrowed her eyes at him. "Listen, pound puppy –" she started but he interrupted her.

"I'm a damn wolf," he growled before stomping away.

"I'm not pregnant," Lucy said, her smile tired. "I wish it were something as simple as that."

Had she just declared pregnancy simple? That was always my worst case scenario when I jumped to a conclusion.

"Then why did you say that to Colt?"

She laughed. "He just rubs me the wrong way, being all gorgeous and demanding and arrogant and freaking sexy."

I joined her laughter. "Welcome to the world of Walkers."

We continued along the path.

"You look tired, Abbs." She reached out to capture my arm and hug me close.

I hadn't been sleeping much, and even though the enlightenment of my Walker powers had given me increased speed, strength and stamina, the dreams were starting to take their toll. I was being tormented by infrequent, but frustrating dreams of the end of First World. Something was trying to give me a message I was yet to figure out.

"Don't change the subject, Luce. What do you have to tell me?" I shook back my long mane of blood-red curls.

I wasn't ready to discuss my dreams, not even with Brace. I had the terrible feeling they were linked to Lucas, the First-World Emperor, and my responsibilities to him. And I had too much to deal with already.

"We should sit down," Lucy said. "And we need total privacy."

Her words restarted my internal freaking out. I led her across to this small inlet of the pond with its own waterfall. The gushing water was loud enough to hide our words. She sat on the rock next to me, her hands clasped in her lap as she stared down at them. I waited, for once striving for patience. Although I might have been slowly going insane on the inside.

She laughed without looking up. "I can feel your urge to reach out and strangle the information from me."

I shrugged. "What can I say? I need to know things. Anything really that's of interest to me. Something tells me your secret is of great interest to me."

"It's bad, Abbs, really bad." She sighed and lifted her eyes to meet my gaze.

My heart was racing.

"Is it Quarn?" I whispered.

My guardian was at the castle with Lucas, helping with the ceremonies for the recently departed Emperor and the crowning of Lucas as the new ruler of First World.

Lucy shook her head. "No, Abbs, stop guessing. You'll never get it right and you're going to drive yourself insane."

I was literally thirty seconds from reaching out and shaking her until she spilled her secret. But just as I lifted my arms she spoke.

"I had a vision about the final battle."

I stilled, the slightest rise of my chest from my shallow breathing my only movement.

"We lost. The Seventine were all free, and they killed everyone but you."

I could hear her words but they sounded like they were coming from far away. I had recently freed the third Seventine to save Brace, but in doing so I broke the lock keeping them from destroying all the worlds. A safeguard that had been instilled by the original seven Walkers. And now Lucy was telling me that my choice would cost everyone's life. She was staring at me, a look of despair etched across her porcelain doll-like features.

"Did ..." I had to clear my throat. "Did you learn anything which could help to change this fate? Surely you had this vision for a reason, so we could learn how to win the final battle."

She laughed out in a hoarse croak. "The first Seventine said that because of your melding with Brace – where you split powers with him – you would never have been strong enough to defeat them."

When we'd first started to talk I'd shut down the connection between Brace and me. In case it was something bad that Lucy didn't want public knowledge. Apparently it was even worse than that. I jumped to my feet.

"Are you telling me that my *unbreakable* bond with Brace is the reason we all die?"

A bond so important that I'd literally made a deal with the devil to reinstate. She nodded, her lips forming a thin line. I just stared at her. The world around me started to spin in a strange dizzying motion. Were the trees closing in?

Lucy opened her mouth again.

"Abby?"

I could see the question on her face as she said my name, but the words were all distorted and echoing. Was I having some type of breakdown? I closed my eyes in an attempt to quell the insanity fluttering around me.

"Abbs!" Her tone was more demanding now.

"I have to tell him," I whispered, opening my eyes. I needed to know what we should do.

"No!" Her response was strong. She waved her hands at me. "You can't tell Brace. My visions indicate that if you reveal this nothing changes."

I shook my head a few times. "I am going to tell him, Luce. I learned something important when I freed the Seventine. Secrets do nothing but cause trouble." I sighed. "It goes against my instincts but I can't save the worlds alone."

And Brace and I were a team. I'd hate for him to keep important information from me.

"Please listen to me," she implored. "He loves you so much. More than anything else, including the worlds. He'll destroy them all to keep you. At least don't tell him straight away."

My heart warmed and swelled at her words, which was odd because my blood felt as if it had turned to ice.

"Have you told anyone else this?" I asked.

"No, Abbs, I haven't said a word."

She was so somber for Lucy. I could see the whirling portal of fear, panic and exhaustion in her blue eyes. And desperation. It was the real emotion blaring at me.

"Okay, Luce, just for now I won't tell him."

It was wrong and I wasn't happy, but I'd give us a little time to try to find a solution.

A few leaves drifted down to rest in our hair. Six months ago we would never have believed it was possible to be sitting in a forest. For almost eighteen years I had been stashed on Earth, in New York, which was urban living at its worst. Derelict buildings, gangs and a compound of abandoned girls. But I was a true First Worlder. And if it was all going to end soon, at least I'd escaped to see my home planet.

"What the hell do I do now?" It wasn't in my nature to roll over and die. I just needed a new plan.

"I don't know," Lucy finally replied.

A burst of energy had me kicking a pile of leaves at her.

"Okay, enough depressing talk. We will not give up. We will continue on the way we started. I'll keep gathering the half-Walkers." I took a deep breath. My voice shook. "And if we don't figure out something better we can try and find a way to break the bond."

Although I knew that would probably kill Brace and me, but if Lucy's vision held true then there was no choice.

Lucy nodded once, the despair evaporating from her features.

"Dammit, you're right. I let that damn vision get to me, but it's not over until I say it is." She jumped to her feet, a fierce determination now overshadowing her words and voice. "Let's head back now. I don't want to miss a moment of this last gathering."

I nodded. I needed to take my place next to Josian. I just hoped I could keep it together. I had to keep my word to Lucy for now and not let Brace know of the vision.

Lucy started to laugh as we walked. "I can't believe you thought I was pregnant."

I chuckled ruefully. "Yeah, I kind of lost my mind for a second there."

Lucy just continued to laugh.

I stared around the stadium. For the first time it was full on all sides; no one wanted to miss this last session. It was easy to see the seven separate sections that housed each Walker clan. There were a few mingling parties but mostly everyone stayed with their own.

I was sitting on the stage elevated in the center; next to me were Talina and Fury. The stage slowly rotated so we had a full-circle view. In front of us were the seven Princeps of each clan, including Brace as interim leader of Abernath. I'd asked Colton and Lallielle to keep an eye on Lucy. I didn't like her out there in this crowd.

Josian stood. As the organizer of this gathering he was heavily involved, and usually ended up as the master of ceremonies of sorts. The almost deafening noise surrounding us eased immediately. One thing Walkers could do was pay attention. And they were huge on respect. Without effort Josian projected his voice out into the massive space.

"Nice to see we made it to day six without an incident." His voice was tinged with humor. It was very obvious that Josian was well liked and respected amongst the other clans. "That's, of course, if we discount the Relli march from yesterday."

Laughter echoed around as everyone was reminded of the march of shame that at least a hundred Relli Walkers had been forced into. It had started as a cross-country challenge: the first team to make it over the five main mountains inside the moonstale zone were the winners.

But some of the Walkers took the task even further, the losers having to march butt naked to the front of every clan zone and declare themselves an 'inferior species'.

Relli lost.

I, of course, only heard about it second-hand from Lucy. Brace had me all but locked inside our tent.

His dark eyes flashed across to me. He must have picked up on the direction of my thoughts. My heart was still heavy. Despite my fighting spirit, Lucy's prediction dominated my mind. But, to keep up appearances, I forced myself to flash him a grin. He wouldn't have to put much pressure on me and I'd tell him; it was what all my instincts were urging anyways.

Josian continued then, breaking the moment between us.

"We all know why we are here. We have exhaustively discussed the Seventine, the release and the half-Walkers. We have demonstrated their powers and how the prophesy made by a soothsayer is starting to evolve."

Josian had decided that we would impart most of the information but we were keeping my conduit abilities under wraps. Although the way Walkers gossiped, the news was probably getting around.

"Now it's your turn. Each clan has gathered and condensed important information. Information that may spell the difference between the success and failure of our half-girls. This is the responsibility of every clan." Josian's voice rose. "Whether you care or not."

More than one Walker had expressed their feeling that this wasn't their problem. Even if the Seventine were all freed these Walkers believed they would be fine. Simply moving on to another star-system. But Lucy's vision of death indicated otherwise.

With a wave of his hand, Josian gestured that Grantham of Relli, his closest friend and supporter, should stand. This was really a formality. As we already knew all the information from Relli.

Grantham's yellow hair shifted in the light breeze. His cat-like green eyes stared out into the mass of silent Walkers.

"Relli have learned of two important facts regarding the Seventine and the original seven. Firstly the Seventine are a machine of sorts. Each part works together to form a complete weapon. Until they are all free their strength is diminished. They can't do anything except sever energy tethers and use this to free their brothers and possess those strong enough."

He had told us this earlier in the week, and it had eased my mind a little. Grantham continued.

"And last night one of our more ... uncommunicative elders approached me."

I sat forward on my seat. This could be new information.

"His grand-leader told him many moons ago that the original seven disappeared because they used a portion of their energy to bind the prison, after this they could no longer exist in their Walker forms. Not while missing these large reserves of energy. So they scattered their remaining power. He believes it lies within the seven half-Walker females."

I glanced at Talina and Fury. They looked both intrigued and surprised. Did we hold the actual energy of the originals?

Grantham sat then and Krahn of Kaos with his caramel-brown colored stripes stood. He moved into the center and spoke without hesitation.

"Kaos members believe a conduit is the way to defeat the Seventine."

I worked hard to keep my expression neutral. Was this a random coincidence or did they know?

"A conduit's mind has the power of creation. It was legend that they could simply imagine what they want or need and it will happen. They can create and sever tethers."

He glanced over to Josian. He had light brown hair, but his eyes were piercing shades of aquamarine.

"You will need to find a conduit to even have a chance of matching power with the complete unit of Seventine. Even if the girls hold original power." He flicked his eyes toward us. "A conduit has to simply imagine what they want, apply enough energy and it will be achieved."

He sat, changing places with Jedi of Gai.

Jedi was short for a Walker with black skin that displayed his white dots beautifully. And even for a Walker he was incredibly handsome.

"Our elders were involved in the imprisonment of the Seventine. There were two safe holds woven into the prison; the first was the blood of an original to free the third." He paused, and I shifted uncomfortably.

No one had really asked what had happened and I wasn't sure if anyone outside our group knew the truth.

"But since that is no longer an option, there's still the ritual of four."

Holy crap! Was there a chance to reverse my weakness? A chance to save my melding bond with Brace? I strained my impressive hearing so I wouldn't miss anything.

"Four originals, or possibly these half-Walker women, if they have original energy, can perform a ritual to send the four freed back into the prison."

He looked directly at me now. "I will give you the ritual information privately."

I crinkled my brow as I stared into his handsome features before giving him a nod. I felt him then. He wanted me to lower my shield. I dropped the energy slightly, letting only his unique power inside. His presence flooded my mind, and his deep timbre tones sounded.

You must combine the blood of the four, sprinkle over the prison and chant the words: invictius collasa repeta intombre.

The words filled my mind and then he added one thing.

And when you question why, find me first.

And just like that he was gone, before I could ask him what he meant. I tightened up my barriers again. Brace was shooting me black eyes. I guessed he didn't like Jedi in my mind.

You guessed right, gorgeous. He's far too popular with the women. We've competed in everything for years. I wouldn't put it past him to try to seduce you.

I laughed. *I'm unseduceable.*

Not in my experience.

His tone lightened, and my heart did its usual flip-flop. For the first time since Lucy's revelation, I felt a little brighter. I had hope now that there was a chance to save my bond.

Tatiana, the only female Princeps, distracted me when she took center stage. She was beautiful with raven dark hair. It was cut short, though, framing her delicate features and making her equally dark eyes look huge. Her voice did not boom but she held everyone captive.

"We have reason to believe that whenever the Seventine are contained again, whether now or after final release, all of the damage they have created will be reversed. Lost life cannot be reverted but severed tethers and objects will return to their original form."

She sat back in her seat. I liked her 'no bull taken or given' attitude. Just simple and to the point.

Since Brace was not truly the Princeps and could add no information, the last speaker was Nos of the clan Whar. He had chestnut hair and these stunning purple eyes, almost the exact shade of his square-patterned marks.

"Our elders learned long ago that the originals always knew the Seventine would free themselves from the prison. They said a chain of events would be swift and unavoidable and that in the end the universe would be thrown into turmoil, but all the worlds would come out better on the other side."

He smiled at us three girls.

"So have faith, half-Walkers, maybe there's nothing you can do but hold on and enjoy the ride."

I didn't smile back.

Josian stood then.

He concluded the event and waved hands for everyone to depart. Final celebrations would be held in the separate clan areas. Walkers were too volatile to spend long in large mixed groups.

And I didn't know about everyone else, but I had a lot to think about after all of that information.

Chapter 3

"Abbs." Lucy found me near my tent in the Doreen area. I was preparing for the night's big celebration. "So that information was interesting," she said with a bright smile.

I couldn't help the returning chuckle. "At least I don't have to think about breaking the bond behind Brace's back. Instead I'll focus on gathering the fourth girl and this ritual."

"You still can't tell him," she warned me again.

"I'll try my best, but he already knows I'm keeping something from him."

I didn't usually have barriers in my mind, so he was curious why there was this small space he couldn't reach.

"It's the fate of seven worlds, Abbs. Don't lose track of the bigger picture."

I glared at her. "I never forget my responsibilities, Lucy. But I still believe that, even if I have to break the bond, it's better that Brace be in on the decision."

"He won't let you." She shook her head. "He'll destroy anyone that tries to take you from him."

I screwed up my face. "You speak about Brace like he's a barbarian. He's incredibly smart and logical. If it comes to it, he'll see the sense."

Lucy snorted. "I've seen what happens, Abby. He's nothing but base, primal instincts when it comes to you." She stepped closer and grabbed my hands. "Trust me."

I stared at the face of my oldest friend. Lucy was like my sister, and for now it didn't hurt to trust her and keep this just between us.

"Okay, fine." I pulled my hands free. "One step at a time. Get out of here, go to Regali, kidnap the fourth half-Walker and then this ritual."

"Sounds like a plan." Lucy bounced around. "Let's go to the party; I'm starving."

I laughed.

Together we left the camping area and walked toward the lake. They had a massive bonfire started. A variety of animal carcasses were roasting over it on large elaborate spits.

"Looks like it's going to be a big night." Lucy laughed. "Walkers do nothing by halves."

I could already see a change in her. When she'd been keeping the secret she'd been tense and nervous. But relieving her burden to me had lifted the weight. I mentally rolled my eyes. Now I was carrying the damn thing. And I hated it.

Suddenly I was swept off my feet. With a shriek I spun my head to see Colton's grinning face.

"Hey, Red, any crazy accusations you want to level on me today?"

I slapped at his arm. "Put me down. And come on, I'm sure that's not your first false pregnancy claim."

He laughed, before stopping dead at a voice behind us.

"You have two seconds to hand me my mate or you'll be shopping for new body parts tomorrow."

I tilted back my head to see the lazy grin of my mate. He was a solid wall of man. Lucy was dwarfed at his side. Turning, Colton threw me straight at Brace, who caught me with ease.

"Hey, baby." He kissed me on the lips. "I'm finally finished Princeps' duty for the tonight. I'm ready to relax."

No one questioned the boys being in Doreen, instead of Abernath. They'd practically been in our area for the entire seven days. Brace set me on my feet before pulling me into the warmth of his body. I was happy to stay snuggled there.

Talina, Fury and Dune wandered up to us then. They each had a glass of something in their hands.

"They're about to do the official toast to end the gathering." Fury grinned, her bright white hair shifting color in the firelight. She lifted the glass to her lips. "And considering this smells a lot like quince, I'm guessing it's going to be a big night."

I snorted, opening my mouth, but Talina beat me to it. "Think you'll manage to keep your shirt on this time, Luce?" she said with a smile.

Lucy didn't miss a beat. "Uh, Talli, remember that I wasn't alone high-kicking on the table."

I laughed. "Yeah, maybe next time I use my dream-projection power I can give everyone a slideshow of the performance. It was pretty unforgettable."

"Sign me up." Colton raised one hand.

"Baby girl.

We all turned as Josian and Lallielle found us. Josian had four cups in his huge tented hands. Lallielle held two.

"You all need drinks," he said as they handed them around to those of us who were drink-less.

Then Josian moved into the firelight.

"Doreen Walkers," he boomed out. "Gather around and grab some crandy."

"Crandy?" I asked Brace.

He grinned. "It's one of the only things that affect Walkers. It's a combination of the juice from a cranberry and a clear liquid from a plant found on Earth."

Leaning my head down, I sniffed at the red liquid in my cup. It had a distinct smell of berry and something else that was sharp and tangy.

"The gathering has been a mammoth effort to try and bring us all together, to prevent the release of the Seventine and the destruction of the First-World star-system."

His blood-red hair glistened in the burning pyre behind him.

"I believe we have moved forward in the right direction. I believe that this did pull us all together as Walkers instead of separate clans, and I have no doubt we'll destroy the threat to us. But for now, let us forget our woes and enjoy one last night Walker-style."

He lifted his glass in the air, and the crowd followed suit. We all raised our drinks and then, with a war cry, it was time to toast. I took a sip and flavors burst onto my tongue. It was bitter and sweet, strong and tart. I swallowed it down, the burning numbness spreading from my lips and following the liquid's path through my body.

"Holy burning hell." I heard Fury gasp. "That's no quince."

Dune laughed. "That's like quince's older, meaner brother."

"Crap, I'm gonna lose my pants this time," Lucy muttered.

Everyone laughed.

Colton reached over and tweaked her on the nose. "I'll look after you, and I never thought I'd say this to a woman, but I'll make sure you keep your clothes on."

Lucy pouted. "Sounds like it's going to be a boring old party."

It wasn't.

The crandy flowed and the mingling began. Along with this there was swimming, gambling, arm wrestling, and more arguing and laughter than I'd ever heard in one place before.

I was on my second drink, sipping it this time because I could already feel a slight fuzziness beating at my mind. I dangled my feet in the edge of the lake. Lucy was next to me. We were watching a drunk Talina kick one Walker after another in a swimming race.

"Hello, beautifuls." A red-faced Walker stumbled down next to us.

"Eff off," Lucy said without even shifting her head to look at him.

He looked confused for a moment. I couldn't wipe the grin off my face as I watched him try to figure out what had just happened. Finally he realized I was staring at him. His eyes widened, jaw dropping as he jumped to his feet, tripping and wobbling around.

"I'm a dead man," he moaned.

"Yes, you are." Colton was the one standing over Lucy and me. "Now run along before the bigger, badder version of me arrives."

"Where's Brace?" I asked. He'd gone to get us more drinks.

"He's been waylaid by a few of the Doreen political leaders. They want to discuss trade alliances between Abernath and Doreen."

I yawned and Colton laughed.

"My sentiments exactly. I hightailed it out of there as soon as the words 'trade agreement' came up." He leaned back between us, his arm curving around Lucy's back.

"Why do you hate all of this stuff so much?" I didn't understand Colton very well.

I noticed Lucy's focus shifting from the water to our conversation. She would want to hear his response.

"My wolf likes things to be less restrictive. He hates that people waste time and effort with false words. And that's all politics are: lies and hidden agendas." Colton shrugged. "Kind of makes me want to rip their faces off."

"Yeah, some friend you are. Abandoning me to them." Brace dropped down next to me, handing over a new glass of crandy.

"Better get used to it, Princeps." Fury gulped down a mouthful as she half sat, half fell onto the ground. "Goooo, Dune." Her screech had us all jumping. She was cheering for the next swimming race.

"He'll never beat Talli," she drawled. "But men have fragile egos. Got to show support."

I snorted.

Brace pulled me closer, his lips nuzzling into the side of my face. "My ego is very fragile," he said. "Do you have anything encouraging to say to me?"

I turned my head until our lips met. "Oh yes, Brace baby, you have a massive ..." I pursed my lips, and he grinned. I lowered my voice. "Really massive ... ego already." I stuck out my tongue. "Enough for two ... maybe three people."

He laughed as he captured my lips. I groaned as he stroked my tongue with his. I could taste the tart cranberry flavor on his lips. Just as our kiss was deepening splashes of icy cold water flickered over us. I gasped, jumping back. Talina and Dune were finished their last swim, both soaking wet and laughing as they joined our group.

"You did great." Fury for once had shelved her snide tone. She threw her arms around Dune. "I'm so proud of you."

Dune grinned at her. "How many glasses have you had? I came dead last and had to be rescued halfway through the race."

She patted him on the arm. "But at least you tried and that's the most important part."

"We should keep Fury permanently drunk," Lucy said, "she's much more agreeable."

"Well, if you're so clever, Lacey, then how about a challenge?" Fury leaned over Dune's knee.

"My name is Lucy, you drunken half-wit," Lucy drawled back.

Although these two were friends, it was complicated.

"And what's your challenge? As long as it doesn't involve the ability to light a fire without wood or a match then I think I'm up for it."

"Okay, then I challenge you to find my father."

Everyone stopped what they were doing and stared at Fury.

"How is that a challenge?" Lucy demanded. "You just want me to do your hard work."

Fury sighed. "No, I honestly can't find him. I don't think he's here."

Dune hugged her close. "I told you that he hid away and became a recluse after he left your mother."

"That's not good enough," Fury snarled. "He abandoned us and my mother wasted away. He needs to know that he took the coward's way out."

"You'll find him one day." Lucy was staring off into the lake again.

Fury opened her mouth but before she could reply a commotion had us spinning around. A group marched into the area. Their presence had the mingling Doreen Walkers parting around them. I found myself pulled to my feet by Brace and I knew why. The group wore masks and robes, black with the tribal marks of Abernath flashing across them. They came to a halt and as one started to chant.

"Oh, for eff's sake," Lucy snarled. "It's an Abernath cult."

Colton stepped closer to Brace. "Tag," he said slapping Brace on the back, "you're up, Princeps."

"What are they chanting?" I murmured.

"They're asking the originals to return and wipe clean the scourge of the worlds," Colton said cheerily.

"And who are the 'scourge'?" I asked, even though I had a good idea.

"Anyone who's not Walker," Brace said. "And of course it has to be the Abernath faction that decided to show up." With a sigh he stepped forward. "Leave now, return to Abernath and when you get there pull your heads out of your asses."

Their chanting cut off. One stepped forward, breaking their formation.

"You're not our chosen Princeps; we don't answer to you." A male voice spoke.

"Long live Que," they all shouted as one.

"Jonathon," Brace drawled. "I've known you for three hundred years. I'm going to recognize your voice."

The man who had spoken shifted uncomfortably. "I don't know what you're talking about."

Brace moved then and faster than we could track he ripped the mask off the front man. He was young with hair of golden browns, and small-set dark brown eyes.

Suddenly a blast of energy shot from the center of the group and hit Brace in the chest. I gasped as he was thrown backwards, landing across the open area. I stepped forward, my rage about to bubble my energy over. But before I could react Brace was at my side. He placed a hand on my arm to stop me.

"They're just stupid kids, Red, I'll deal with them."

I snorted. Anyone less than four hundred was a kid to him.

Jonathon lifted his arms then. "We didn't mean harm. It's just our duty to spread the words of the originals."

This had to be the group that had been harassing Lucy and us half-Walkers during the entire gathering.

"I'll give you one chance to leave." Josian stepped forward with a few Doreen elders. "If we have to ask again, you won't be leaving in a conscious state."

The group hesitated, but as they glanced between Josian, Brace and Colton they must have decided they were outmanned. With one last glance, Jonathon reached down to grab his hood.

"If I hear of your extremist actions again," Brace called after them, "I'll exile you from Abernath. Keep that in mind."

"You don't know who we are," one of the hooded said.

Brace grinned. "But I know Jonathon and I know how to make him talk."

"Squeal like a bitch actually," Colton added. "Might be fun."

They were just turning to leave when suddenly Jonathon turned back to us and started to speak. But this time his voice was different, flat, as if he were reciting a speech.

"Children of Gods, born unknown and alone,
the seven are needed to eliminate. Take heed,
for baby will not live till four and one year
unless removed from the world here.
The youngest and strongest to collect.
Lost and alone, a god-man is the key.
Gather the halflings, stone and fear.
The end of days is written in mineral. "

"Oh, eff," Lucy said, "that's the prophesy from Frannie, right?"

I nodded, trying to figure out what was happening.

He continued to repeat it over and over and suddenly he added a few words to the end. Words which were not in English.

"What did he say?" I asked Brace, an edge of panic in my tone. I was getting one of my bad feelings about this.

"He added two extra lines to the end," Brace said, his tone short. *"Death is near and will come on swift winds, unless the first half meets a fiery end. "*

"First half? That's me, right?" I attempted to

swallow the huge lump in my throat.

Suddenly Jonathon flung his hands forward. He was still chanting and from his finger tip these red and yellow sparks emerged. I had to look twice because the first time I hadn't realized that the spark was actually solid, until it shot toward me with the force of a missile and hit my shoulder with a thud that knocked me backwards.

"Detain him." I heard Brace order before he dropped to my side. "Josian, is that what I think it is?"

His expression wasn't giving me much hope that this was nothing to worry about.

"The scepter of Klaus," Josian muttered.

I was about to start yelling, demanding someone tell me what the hell was sticking out of my arm, when I felt it beneath my lace marks. My blood started to pulse, and it burned suddenly, as if my very skin was on fire.

"What's happening?" I gasped out.

"The scepter was a weapon developed early on by the Seventine. I thought the originals destroyed it all." Josian looked panicked.

"What does it do?" Lucy all but shrieked.

Josian ran his hand through his hair in an agitated manner. "When they knew that they couldn't kill an original they found this. It literally turns a Walker to stone. A living statue."

"Keep her heart beating," Brace bit out. "I know Que still held a few bottles of the cure."

"But you can't leave," Talina said, sitting close by, a few tears running down her face. "The moonstale is up for another ten hours."

"She doesn't have ten hours." Brace stood abruptly. "Just keep her heart beating."

I couldn't feel my left arm anymore. The burning was lessening, but so was any sensation there.

"Stay with me, baby girl," Josian said from one side. "Your mother and I will feed you our energy to fight the spread."

My parents each took my hands, although I couldn't feel anything anymore. I just lay there watching their perfect faces shimmering under the moonstale dome. Warmth started to spread through me again, and I could feel the warring within my blood. And then Josian's lace marks flickered a few times before disappearing. Noise erupted around us in a huge conglomeration of sound. The moonstale had fallen.

"Brace is badass," Lucy said.

And then in that moment Josian's mark reappeared. Brace must have figured out a way to disable the dome to allow him enough time to open a doorway. I mentally urged him to hurry. My parents were helping but the loss of sensation was still slowly creeping along my body.

"Her marks have stopped swirling," Fury snapped out. "Brace better move his butt."

The words continued over me as everyone spoke, but my ears seemed to have suddenly stopped working right. I kept missing parts of the conversation. And then the burning sensation moved to my eyes, and I couldn't move them around any longer. My stare was locked on my father's face as he continued to pour his energy into me. I guessed I looked calm on the outside, considering I couldn't move my face anymore, but on the inside I was screaming. The claustrophobic sensations ripped through me. I was unable to move my body, but was still aware of my surroundings.

Josian moved out of my line of sight and my desperation grew. Now I could see nothing but the darkness of the First-World sky. How much longer until I was a statue? At this desperate thought, Brace was there, filling my view. A dash of hope flared. He leaned close to me, his lips moving, but I caught none of what he said. Except the last word. Sorry.

Oh, crap.

Something struck me hard, right in my chest above my heart. The fact I felt anything at all told me the force used. And then I was on fire. If I'd thought the burning sensation before was painful that was only because I didn't have this new pain as a comparison. My skin was charring off my bones, lava flowed through my veins and embers repeatedly stabbed through my body.

I screamed, or attempted to, but no sound emerged. And then when I was mid-wail my screams started to echo around. My vocal cords were free; the paralysis was starting to wear off. Whatever Brace had done was working. Halting my wails, I gritted my teeth and rode out the pain.

"You're doing great, Abbs, it's almost over now."

I could finally hear Brace's voice and the sound was more soothing to my pains than anything else would have been. And then I could feel his warm hand wrapped around mine. Piece by piece my body became my own again, until finally I was able to stand.

Lucy ran at me, wrapping her arms around me tightly. Talina was right behind her and then on a very unusual note Fury was the last to join our group hug.

"I thought you were gone," Lucy said, her voice muffled. "Your skin went this stunning shade of gold, but I could see the life disappearing from you."

"Don't do that again," Fury bit out as she pulled back. "Us halves need our fearless leader."

I laughed then. "Okay, I'll try not get hit by some weird, ancient unheard-of rock and turn to stone. Seriously, how many times in one life could that happen?"

"You'd be surprised." Colton grinned. He was standing next to Brace.

Taking two steps, I threw my arms around Lallielle and, as always, Josian joined in. I could hear him muttering about gray hair again. When he pulled back he addressed the many Doreen members who were gathered around us.

"I think it might be time to call it a night," he started. "Brace and I have a few Abernaths to deal with."

I could see five of them standing to the right of us, their hoods still in place and Doreen men around them, keeping them in place. The rest must have escaped in the uproar.

"I'll take Red to our tent and make sure she's fine. Don't start without me." Brace's words were tense. He was not happy, his eyes black as pitch, and I wouldn't like to be in those Abernaths' robes when he got to them.

We moved through the dispersing crowd, and I had to say I felt completely fine, as if nothing had happened.

"You're trying to give me a heart attack, Abigail. I didn't think I'd make it in time." He pulled me closer.

I looked up into his face. "What would have happened if you hadn't? Is it permanent?"

"I've never known anyone to come back once the heart is frozen. The curative liquid only works if the organ can still pump it around."

My blood chilled again at the thought that I had almost become a living statue.

"Thank you," I said softly. "I don't know how you managed to break the dome, but I'm so glad you could."

Brace managed to laugh. "Don't ask. I'll probably be in shit over that soon. Worth it, though."

We reached the tent and Brace made sure I was safely inside on our blow-up bed. "Don't leave; I need to know you're safe, just for five minutes." His expression pleaded. "Please."

"I'll be right here waiting for you," I promised.

He hesitated, before a grin crossed his features and he reluctantly moved out of the door. "See you soon, Red."

My pulse raced as I watched him leave. I couldn't wait for him to return.

Chapter 4

The next morning I felt great as I got ready to travel to Regali, the ominously dubbed 'planet of the beasts'. Colton's sister, Magenta, had been there before and, using her knowledge, Colton was going to open a doorway into the jungle of Artwon. Apparently this was the most likely place to find the half, as it was the most densely populated.

I'd traced from the field to my room in Angelisian the moment the moonstale dome had fallen on the gathering. My head was pounding a little, but I seemed to have recovered pretty quickly from the previous night. Brace and Josian had not gleaned much information from the Abernaths. They didn't seem to really know anything of importance. And Brace was sure that

Jonathon had no idea how he'd come to possess the scepter of Klaus.

I was in my closet, just collecting a few essential clothing items, when I felt Josian's presence enter my room. I was getting much better at not just sensing the energy, but also individualizing it to fit with its owner. I popped my head out of the wardrobe door.

"Dad." I smiled as familiar bronze eyes locked on me. "What's up?"

He stood straighter, his ivory skin glowing softly as always. "I know you're in a hurry to gather the next girl, and try that ritual for the four, but we have to do one thing before you leave."

I tilted my head to the side, waiting for him to continue.

"Lucas is to be inaugurated tomorrow night at dusk. All of us have been requested to attend."

I attempted to keep my expression calm, despite the tumultuous storm brewing inside. Lucas' father had died a little over a week ago, a debilitating immune disease taking its final toll. After the days of mourning and farewells for Emperor Christian, it was now time for his son to take the throne. Lucas was a friend of sorts, but a friend who wanted more. He believed I was his destined Empress, despite my clear melding bond with Brace, and at times it made for tension and awkwardness. But he would expect our attendance and I owed him that much respect.

"Okay," I finally said. "I guess we can delay another day."

What I really wanted to say was: hell no. But First World was my home and I needed to make sure I didn't piss Lucas off too badly. Josian grinned. He couldn't read my guarded thoughts, but my expression probably gave me away.

"We'll take the buggies to the castle tomorrow morning. Lucas has also requested no doorways or tracing with so many people around," Josian said, his tone dry.

Walker's didn't like orders, even if they were phrased as polite requests.

After Josian had left me to finish my packing, I opened my mind to Brace. I already missed him and he'd only been away on Abernath for a few hours. He was trying to help maintain a semblance of order, and assist in the decision for appointing the next Princeps.

Something told me it was going to be Brace and there was nothing we could do to stop it. He had told me he didn't want the position because he would be gone so much. But I had encouraged him. If nothing came of the ritual for the four I had no choice but to break the bond, so maybe a little distance was for the best. My heart tightened inside my chest, as if someone had reached in and grasped it tightly before slowing squeezing the life out of it.

Red.

His voice washed over me. I quickly locked the negative thoughts away.

Are you okay?

I hadn't quite hidden everything. He could feel my worry.

Yep, just missing you like crazy.

I poured all of my love into those words, without even meaning to.

I'd much rather be with you than trying to wrangle these Walkers. I swear not one of them can make a decision without ten hours of discussion.

He paused.

Well, in regards Princeps, there seems to be no doubt about who they want.

I sighed. *They chose you, didn't they?*

I felt him hesitate. *Yes.* He paused again. *But I haven't accepted yet.*

Why?

Because it's a big job. Not always, of course, as you can see from Josian. Walkers manage themselves mostly fine, but someone has to sort out the mess Que made ... I'm going to be gone a lot.

I swallowed, working hard to remind myself that this is what I wanted.

You should take it, Brace. You were born to be Princeps, and frankly you'd make an amazing leader. You're a little hot-headed, but if you get that under control ...

He snorted. *I'm only like that with you, Red. Most of the time I'm cool as ice.*

I felt his attention shift.

Baby, I have to go now. A problem and an idiot have both come to my attention.

Tell Colton hey.

Brace laughed. *See you tomorrow at Lucas' inauguration. Be good and I love you.*

I felt him withdraw from my mind. My heart lifted at the thought of seeing him the next day. I was glad he was going to be there for the ceremony. I had no idea how I was going to survive breaking the bond. Even when the Seventine had possessed him, there'd still been a bond between us, and it was still the worst pain I'd ever felt. I clenched my fists. This ritual had to work.

"Abbs?" Lucy's voice broke me from my thoughts.

I turned my head as she walked into my room.

"Have you heard from Brace?" She flopped onto my bed.

She looked tired. I knew her vision was keeping her up at night. And she wasn't the only one.

I sauntered closer to her. "Why do you ask?" I paused at the edge of my bed, staring down at her.

She shrugged. "No reason, I just recognize that desolate look on your face."

I laughed.

She sat up straighter, her glare nailing me.

I returned it with my own stare. "You don't fool me, Lucy. You want to know if Colt is coming tomorrow."

She huffed, her brows narrowing over her eyes. "Please, I don't care what that mangy mutt is doing. It's simply a community service to know whether I have to call animal control."

"I think maybe your overkill on the dog jokes indicates something deeper than that. What happened last night between you two?"

She flopped back on the bed, closing her eyes. "Nothing," she mumbled. "Absolutely nothing."

I was reaching out to shake the living crap out of her – she was being deliberately obtuse – when Talina popped into my room.

"I have some news," she burst out.

Lucy and I spun in her direction.

"I'm going to stay here and help Josian and Lallielle search the dark mountains."

We stared at her for a minute.

"I know I wanted to go to Regali with you both, but I need to help search." She huffed in a breath. "I have a strange feeling about these mountains."

"Fair enough," I said, trusting Talina's judgment. "I hope we're quick finding this next girl, then we can come back and help you search."

"What do you know about Regali?" she asked, dropping onto the bed next to Lucy, her luxurious emerald hair spreading out around her. "Do you have a game plan?"

I shrugged, shifting from foot to foot. "Nah, you know me: just show up and see what happens. It's apparently a very intense jungle, this Artwon."

"Yes," Lucy interrupted, "we're more worried about snakes and spiders."

Talina nodded, her lids half closed. I knew she would have no idea what Lucy was talking about; they had different predators on Spurn. But she agreed anyways.

"Where's Fury?" I asked.

"She's with Grantham. He's helping her with her energy. They definitely have complementary powers and already after a few sessions she's getting stronger," Talina said, her words reminding me of Fury's insatiable need to increase her fire power.

I was also reminded of my own need for improvement.

"We need to try my tethering again. With that tip from the Walker about conduit power, we might just have a shot at controlling the energy," I said.

Talina nodded, sitting up and facing me. I was dying to test out this conduit skill. It would be useful to know if I could use my mind to create and destroy.

"Yes! We have to be so strong that we can call on the power at any moment and fully utilize all of our individual strengths." Talina's brown eyes flared with a determined light. "Let's go now."

We stood facing the ocean, the grass under our feet a vibrant lime green. The water splashed in its tumult of blues, the majesty, as always, taking my breath away.

"You ready?" Talina turned her head to face me.

Taking in a lung full of the salty air, I nodded. From the corner of my eye I noticed Lucy drop down onto the ground. She was our run-for-help girl.

The air shifted around us as Talina called her energy and the water surrounded her. I flung forward my golden cord and, without any physical contact needed, a strand flew from the center of the water spout and we were tethered together.

So you don't have to touch us. Talina's voice held a curious wonder. *Let's see what else we can do.*

The Walker had said my mind and energy were the key to controlling this tethering. That if I simply visualized what I wanted, I could manifest it.

Josian had said this was unheard of, even from the original Walkers. The ability to create and destroy on that level was the domain of the lalunas alone; not Walkers.

I could see the golden thread attached to the watery center. I tugged on it again and, as before, it simply stretched out.

What are you going to do? Talina asked as she watched me. She stood calmly, knowing she had no control over what I was doing.

I laughed. *I have no idea. I'm going to picture an axe or sharp object and use it to cut the cord.*

What about scissors?

I paused. That could work.

It took very little effort now to manipulate my energy and it no longer scared me. At some point my power and I had formed an understanding and there was an almost co-dependent bond between us.

I mentally shaped a very sharp pair of scissors, and strangely enough they appeared before us in almost a ghostly specter. I directed them toward the tether.

Closing my eyes, I forced the blades of power shut. An explosion flashed and my eyes flew open in time to see a massive shimmering wall of energy form between Talina and me. Her eyes widened and at that moment we were blasted apart. I flew backwards. It felt like the wall was slammed against my body, pushing me. And if the force didn't abate soon, I was going to hit the house. I noticed then that the cord tethering me to Talina had not fully been severed; it had only partly disconnected.

And if I wasn't mistaken the partially broken golden cord was the sparking, fizzing force pushing me back.

I formed my scissors again and, using more of my energy, I surrounded the cord and forced the blades to close. Screaming out with more of my strength, I finally heard the clink of the metaphorical power scissors as they cut those final strands. The wailing wall of energy died and I hit the ground with a hard thud, the final force sending me into the front window of our house.

I braced myself as the glass shattered around me. I could feel the jagged points cutting through my shirt and into my back and sides. A scrape burnt along my cheek. The piercing pain started at my lips and continued up past my eye. I wanted to scream. The pain was agonizing as glass punctured along my body, ripping through my delicate skin.

Finally I stopped moving. I was in the front meeting room, my blood spraying around the white carpet and walls like some macabre painting. I shuddered, my body shaking as I fought the urge to collapse. I knew the glass still littered my body and I really didn't want to push it in further.

"Aribella, don't move." My father's voice sounded from the back doorway.

"Wasn't planning on it," I croaked out, my voice shaking.

I heard more movement behind me, followed by a gasp which definitely came from my mother.

"Do something," Lallielle murmured.

Damn, what could they see, besides the ton of blood I was dumping on the floor?

Lucy's horrified face appeared on the outside of the broken window. Behind her was a dripping wet Talina.

"Glad to see you had water to cushion your fall and not a damn house." I shuddered more.

Lucy practically dived through the window then. I flinched as she snatched at my face. I couldn't stop the cry from escaping my lips and I let my mental shield fall briefly as the burning pain lashed at my face again.

"I'm so sorry, Abbs. The cut was closing in over the glass in your face. I didn't know what else to do." Her face fell as she stared at me.

In her hand she clutched a large jagged shard, the blood dripping from it in a slow hypnotic manner. Glancing down, she finally seemed to notice the object in her hand, and with a small cry she thrust it away from her, flinging it into the corner of the room.

I took a deep breath before smiling at my shell-shocked friend, although the best I could managed was a bit of a wonky, though hopefully reassuring, lip curl.

"No harm, Luce, I just wasn't expecting that."

I realized that there were similar sharp burns along my back.

"I've managed to get most of the glass out before your skin healed." Josian spoke over my shoulder, explaining the pain. "Your mother's gone for the medical kit to help me with the rest."

I froze even more. I hated pain and something told me this was going to hurt.

We were all distracted then as a doorway opened on the front lawn. Josian moved to stand in front of the broken window, his massive frame practically shielding all of us from view. But I knew immediately who it was.

His energy signature was unique and actually quite similar in strength to the wall of power that had flung me into the house.

Brace had arrived.

Josian stepped back to my wounded self, leaving a clear view outside.

Brace wasn't alone. Colton almost shoved him out of the way as they moved in long-legged strides across the grass. Brace's black eyes were locked on me. He looked pissed off, but more than that he was worried. Through the shared part of our bond I could feel the icy tendrils of fear from him. He'd known I was hurt but until right that moment, when he could actually see me, he hadn't known how bad it was.

Colton reached Lucy's side. "What happened?" he snapped at her.

Lucy wrinkled her brow as she stared up at him. "I'm sorry – what?"

He looked a little confused as he repeated his question, this time with less bite. Again Lucy simply stared up at him, her face still scrunched up. Finally she turned to me.

"Do you understand what he's saying? All I'm getting is bark, bark, growl."

Talina and I both snorted. Pain shot through me as I moved and I couldn't help the little groan.

Colton grinned then. Leaning down, he flicked out his tongue and traced it from her chin up to the corner of her mouth. Lucy gasped, her eyes widening and her jaw falling open.

"Since you clearly expect me to greet you like a wolf," Colton drawled.

She blinked twice. "Just try to stop yourself before you sniff my butt," she finally said.

She moved back then to crouch next to me, just out of the reach of my blood pool.

"I'm pretty sure I just had my first real sexual experience," she murmured, leaning near my ear.

I grinned, taking in her shocked expression. My crazy friend was not usually caught off guard. I shifted, wincing as the pain blasted under my skin again. It felt as if my body was trying to expel the glass.

I held out my hand. I needed Brace right then. I was hurting and I could tell that he was about to lose his shit.

He didn't push anyone aside; they simply moved out of his way. He crouched before me, clearly not caring that my blood was soaking into his black pants. He wore a type of ceremonial cape, black like the pants, embroidered with silver decals and this intricate shield. His marks were perfect. Pulsing gold threaded along the dark tribal pattern. The gold was part of our melding bond.

"Damn, what did you run out on?" I smiled, hoping to see some brown bleed back into his eyes.

Colton snorted. "Nothing important, just the ceremony to accept his role as Princeps."

Brace spun his head and nailed Colton with a glare. "It was just a discussion on the possibility. I would never have an official crowning without Red."

Colton tilted his head in that way that always reminded me he was a wolf. "Still, there were a few surprised faces as he jumped up in the middle of Canon's boring as hell speech, opened a doorway and quick as anything disappeared."

"Couldn't have been that quick. You were on my ass the whole way here," Brace muttered.

"If you were escaping, so was I. I hate all that ceremony stuff."

I noticed for the first time how casually Colton was dressed. Just shorts and a fitted blue t-shirt, the same icy blue color as his eyes. Very different from the darkly formal Brace.

"What happened here?" Colton asked the question again.

Talina was the one who explained about our little experiment. Brace never took his eyes off me. At some point Lallielle had also returned. She was crouched on my other side, concern in her green eyes.

"So now Abby's skin has healed over the remaining glass?" Lucy asked, her face falling.

Josian took a deep breath. "Yes, I'm going to have to open her wounds again."

"Do it." I nodded. "Do it now before I freak out."

Turmoil clouded Brace's eyes. He reached out and took my hand, pulling it toward him until it rested against his heart. My mother had my other hand clutched in hers.

I'm here, baby. Just focus on my heartbeat. Stay here in our minds so I can shield you.

I gulped, trying to follow Brace's advice, but all I could think about was what Josian was about to do back there. And when he was going to make the first cut.

"I can't look," Lucy said. "The last thing Abbs needs is me barfing on her."

I was distracted then as the first touch of cold steel hit near my lower spine. I tensed, which only made it worse as the blade bit into my skin. My hands clenched as I gritted my teeth and tried to escape.

I'm here, let me shield you.

How? I practically begged, tears welling in my eyes.

His power burst into me, surrounding my mind with the strength and warmth of his will. The surge was unexpected and my own power rose to mingle with its mate. By the time I surfaced again, opening my eyes, Josian was speaking.

"I'm almost done, baby girl, just two more."

Whatever Brace had done, I'd missed most of the agony.

Thank you, I mouthed at him. His eyes softened, his free hand reaching up to push back my loose curls.

The steel touched me again. I bit back a moan, looking around for a distraction.

"Where's Lucy?" I asked Colton, who was leaning against the wall.

Talina was sitting next to him.

"She passed out."

"Shut up," Lucy interrupted him, her head popping up from the white couch. "I was just having a nap. I needed my five minutes' beauty sleep."

"Done," Josian said.

I heard the clink of steel hitting something.

Josian reached around and kissed me on the cheek. "You were brave."

I laughed weakly. "Trust me, I was a big girl on the inside."

"Let me clean you up," Brace said.

He scooped me up in his arms. I clutched at my shirt to stop it from falling off me.

I felt no pain as Brace held me close. Now that the glass had been removed, my Walker healing had fixed me right up.

"Don't forget to be back here early for Lucas' thing," Lucy said, her voice tinged with sarcasm and what sounded a little like envy.

"Yes, it's late now. You should rest until the morning." Lallielle stepped forward to kiss my cheek. "Love you, darling."

"I love you too," I said, blowing a few random kisses around the room.

I felt like sharing the love. In fact, I kind of wanted to jump and sing and dance.

"What's wrong with me?" I shook my head a few times.

Brace laughed. "It's the energy-high from me, kind of a similar experience to drinking alcohol, but without the hangover."

Colton sighed. "Once there was this princess from Egypt and … well, let's say the energy-high was only the start of the fun."

Lucy punched him straight in the ribs. He actually stopped what he was saying and looked down.

"Holy shit. You punch like a man. What the fu _"

She interrupted him again. "Shut your hole, wolf-man."

"Despite the fact you finally got the wolf part right, you're the most frustrating female I've ever met." He threw his hands in the air. He did that a lot around us.

Lucy pulled out a large white bone from behind her. Where the hell had she hidden that?

"Fetch." She tossed it through the broken window.

In an almost involuntary motion, Colton's eyes flicked out toward the grassed area. Everyone in the room broke down in laughter. Even Josian chuckled a few times.

Colton closed his bright, icy-blue eyes briefly. As he opened them, the wickedest grin crossed his face. "How long have you been waiting to do that?"

Lucy just grinned.

Colton leaned in closer to her. "I'm going to enjoy punishing you for that one." He said it quietly but I heard him.

"In. Your. Dreams," Lucy said.

"Red and I are going to leave now. Are you staying for the ceremony, Colt?" Brace asked.

The blond Walker nodded.

"Maybe they can come with us to the snow house," I said with fake enthusiasm.

I really wanted alone time with Brace. Except a part of me insisted on reminding me that if the ritual didn't work I needed to start distancing myself from Brace. And if we were alone I wasn't sure I could keep the secret from him. My instincts urged me to tell him everything.

"Sure," Brace said, the strangest look crossing his masculine features. "If that's what you want."

Lucy jumped in with enthusiasm. "Yes! Right. Let's do this. I've been dying to see the house under the stars."

"Okay, well change into warm clothes. Meet us all back here in five," I said.

Everything okay, Red?

I was in my closet, pulling on some new jeans when Brace spoke to me. His tone was curious, maybe a tad worried. I quickly threw on a shirt, jacket and some boots before stepping out.

"Everything is great," I said, moving across the large space and into his arms. My cuts were all healed up so I had no discomfort.

Actually, everything really sucked. I hated lying to him. In fact I hated lying period, but it was even worse with my mate. I wanted to tell him so badly, but we were talking about the end of seven worlds and, according to Lucy, Brace wouldn't make the same choice as me. My hope was that the ritual would work. If it didn't … then I had to have faith that breaking the melding bond wouldn't kill us both. And after the final battle was all over, if we survived, we could be melded mates again.

Brace was watching the changing emotions cross my face. I tried to school my features into lines of ease. I don't think I fooled him.

"You don't have to keep things from me, Abby. We're partners. We face life's obstacles together; you never have to deal with them alone again." His words sent warmth and icy fear down my spine.

This was why my instincts were screaming so loudly to tell him. But I couldn't break my word to Lucy … well, not yet, anyways.

We were quiet as we made our way into the front room; Brace kept my hand firmly grasped in his. Stepping through the door, I could see that someone had attempted to clean up the mess, although the blood stains weren't going anywhere. Talina, Lucy and Colton trailed back into the room, all wearing warm clothing.

My parents gave out hugs and together we stepped through a doorway into the cold, beautiful night world.

"Shut-the-freaking-door," Lucy said as she stood there, flakes drifting around her face. "I want one; get me one now."

I laughed. "Better find yourself a Walker and someone who knows how to wield a hammer."

She smiled, just the briefest grin, and to her credit didn't glance at Colton. But from the corner of my eye I could see his eyes were locked firmly on her face.

We were going to have trouble there. No doubt.

Chapter 5

People were everywhere, and the noise was intense. It was time for the Emperor inauguration, and streams of First Worlders were filling the large throne room. I shifted uncomfortably in the hard-backed chair, bored already. After a lovely night around the fireplace, and sleeping with my love in my room under the stars, I was now sitting with a numb butt waiting for this stupid ceremony. The castle throne room had been set up with seats surrounding the ornate cathedral chairs, although these were empty at the moment.

"Remind me why we're here again?" Lucy said around the biggest yawn I'd ever seen. Her eyebrows practically disappeared into her hairline.

"Because we're Lucas' friends," Talina admonished us. She'd always been the closest to him.

"And because we made First World our home base," Lallielle added. "We must respect this world and its customs."

I pasted a smile on my face, knowing they both had a point. I just found all this ceremony stuff and politics quite silly and a waste of time. Time which could be better spent on other things. But at the end of the day we did owe Lucas this.

"Do they feed us after?" Fury shifted from where she was a few seats down from me.

Dune and she had met us at the beach house that morning. She'd been raving about training with Grantham. Apparently she had new fire moves to show me.

"Lucas will have a dance and banquet after the inauguration." Josian's voice boomed in the echoing hall.

A few of the impeccably dressed people around us gave him a glare, but would never say anything to the imposing Walker.

"Thank the gods, I'm starving," Fury muttered.

She was always extra hungry after using her fire.

"I won't be staying," I said bluntly. "I have to get to Regali; we're running out of time. I need the fourth girl to try that ritual. It might be our last chance to stop all seven being released."

"Do you need us to go with you?" Fury asked.

I shook my head. "No, Lucy and I will just go quickly and grab the next half."

Fury snorted. "Oh, yeah, 'cause we're always so compliant."

"If I got you to leave, the rest should be more than easy." I raised my brows.

And she shrugged, apparently agreeing with that sentiment.

Talina jumped in then. "I'm staying to help search the mountains. I think there's something very sinister hidden under there and I feel that Josian will need all the help he can get. You and Dune should come to the mountains too."

It looked to me as if Josian was going to protest, but in the end he simply smiled, his bronze eyes facing forward to the middle of the room where the two throne chairs rested.

Fury sighed. "Always something to clean up with these Seventine. Count us in; I'm ready to exterminate them and their minions."

"So, just you and me, sister," I said to Lucy. "Like the old days."

"Uh, did you forget about us?" Colton popped his blond head around Brace, who sat on my left side. "You need my doorway to get you to the right place. Plus there's no way young Brace here would let you jet off to another world without him, and where he goes, I go."

Lucy nodded, her face serious. "I have heard that dogs are a man's best friend. It's good that you're staying true to your nature."

Brace snorted, his hand shooting out to cover Colton's mouth before he retaliated.

"Are you going to tell me yet what's up with you and Colt?" I side-whispered to Lucy.

She'd been extra snappy with him since the last night of the gathering, even during the relaxed atmosphere at the snow cabin.

"I don't want to talk about it here. Can I show you in my head?" Her voice was very low.

I paused. "You're a soothsayer. I can't breech your mind to see anything."

She shifted a little closer to me. "I think I've figured out a way to project outside my own head."

I turned my face to the right so I could see her better. I was about to open my mouth and ask how when suddenly there were images in my mind. It was similar to the time I had infiltrated Lallielle's mind, almost like a movie screen. I recognized the scenery, but the memories weren't mine.

Lucy stood in the spot near the waterfall, back in the Doreen area at the Walker gathering. She was alone, the moonlight shining down on her blond curls. I would guess it was late at night, and despite the fact Lucy wasn't supposed to be wandering alone, she'd clearly ignored that warning because I could see no one around her. It must have been after the Abernaths entered our area, when I was back in my tent.

"What are you doing out here?" She spoke without turning her head.

At first I couldn't see who she was talking to, until he stepped out to join her in the moonlight. Colton. His hair even more white-blond than hers. He towered over her, casting her in his shadow.

"You know you're not supposed to be out here. It's not safe." For once he sounded serious.

Lucy laughed. "The position of gorgeous, annoying mother hen has already been taken by Abby."

Geez, thanks, Lucy. Biatch.

"So why are you here?" He moved even closer, until he was right up in her personal space.

"Why do you care?" she shot back at him.

He stopped then; the look on his face was odd.

"Don't confuse my interest as anything more than a casual question between friends." His voice was cold now. In fact his entire demeanor had changed. All his warmth was gone. "We'll never be anything more."

Lucy's face flew up, stormy eyes clashing with his icy blue. "I don't understand … what did I do?" For a split second her vulnerability shone through.

Colton's features softened. "It's not you. You … damn, you're perfect." He said each word as a statement. "But, I'm broken. And before you get that crazy chick gleam in your eyes, it's not broken like you could fix me." He looked away from her. "I don't even have all the pieces anymore."

Lucy opened her mouth, but instead of speaking she simply stared up at Colton. He was watching the large moon. I saw her swallow a few times before she spoke again.

"So are you trying to tell me that you will never have a girlfriend or mate?" Lucy said.

"Not one that matters to me," he said in a low, rough tone. "Go back to your tent," he finally ordered before walking away.

Lucy stood there for a few more moments. A single tear ran down her cheeks.

"Damn him," she muttered.

The woods disappeared.

I came back to the throne room when Lucy stopped the memories. I turned to her.

"Is that something other soothsayers can do?" I asked, my voice low and shocked. "My barriers did nothing to keep your memories out." Could she infiltrate anyone's mind like that?

"I accidentally discovered it during training. Lallielle told me she'd never heard of it happening with Francesca. I meant to tell you but forgot in the excitement of the gathering. I've practiced a few times, but only kind of figured it out on the last night of the gathering."

I felt the slightest grin cross my face. "This might be very useful. Sometimes talking isn't always possible. How far away can you project into a mind?"

"A few miles was no problem ..." she started, her words trailing off as a trumpeting fanfare blared from somewhere behind us.

It looked like the ceremony was about to begin.

Do you know what Colton was talking about? I knew Brace had been watching in my head.

There are many dark secrets in Colton's family. He'll tell you when he's ready, but warn Lucy: it's going to be a battle taming his wolf.

I had really hoped that Lucy wouldn't get dragged into Colton's mess. But judging by her emotional reaction that hope might be a little too late.

A side door opened. I caught the movement from my peripherals and turned toward it. Out marched the seven mayoral leaders of First World. I remembered them from my last visit to the castle, including the squat and unattractive Mayor Rhys Johansson. He had that smirk on his face again, the kind of smug, self-satisfied expression that made me want to punch him in the mouth.

They were all dressed in floor-length red robes. Hoods rose up behind them to form large cones that towered above their hairline. The music rose to a crescendo as they neared the throne chairs.

My heart rate increased; I had no idea why I was reacting so much to this but the feeling in the air was indescribable. Almost like little buzzes of electricity coated my skin. I shifted forward on my seat, my eyes locked on the center of the room.

The seven mayors spread out to stand in the semi-circle. Each of them faced toward our end of the room. We had the best seats; those behind wouldn't see much of the action.

And then another man walked alone down the long carpet. He had a dark, caramel-colored skin, a shaved head and was at least a head taller than any of the mayors. He carried a large purple silken pillow, and resting on top was the red royal stone, the other half to my laluna. As if it read my mind, the blue stone was suddenly in my hand. Its sparkles drew the attention of my family.

"Is it here for the ceremony?" I leaned out to whisper at Josian.

His face looked thoughtful. "It hasn't appeared for the last few Emperor inaugurations. Either it's simply here for you, or Lucas is going to be a powerful leader."

"Should I take it up to rest with its pair?" I asked.

Josian was opening his mouth to speak when the room went deadly silent. The music cut off mid-beat and I sucked in a deep breath and held it in anticipation. My hand tightened on my stone.

The handsome man from earlier had lain the pillow in between the two throne chairs and was now seated on a nearby bench. I was startled to realize Quarn sat next to him. I waited a few moments to catch my guardian's eye, but he seemed to be very preoccupied, keeping a close watch on everything.

"It's starting." Brace leaned to my ear and spoke.

I transferred the stone, and with my free hand I reached out and took Brace's hand. I swung my head around as the slamming of a door echoed through the room. This must have been the signal for the music to resume.

It was different this time, softer but with a catchy melody. Everyone in the room stood as Lucas finally stepped into the space of the open double doors. He was again dressed in white and gold, but his clothing was so much more ornate than the previous time I had seen him.

"It's a wonder that the man can walk with that much bling," Lucy muttered.

And she wasn't kidding. Jewels started at the collar and continued pretty much to the floor. In a strange contrast, on his head rested only a small wreath of gold leaves. Not the sort of crown I would expect for the Emperor.

That's the Emperor-in-waiting crown. It'll be replaced by the crown jewels during this ceremony.

Oh, yeah, that makes sense.

Brace sounded amused. *He'll be lucky to be able to hold his head up.*

I watched as Lucas made the slow progression to the center of the room. He stopped and greeted many along the way. From somewhere a woman stepped out between the throne chairs; she carried another pillow and this one held the crown. I studied her closely. There was something familiar about her young features. Her long black hair and green eyes were like Lallielle's.

"That's Jinissara, a relative of yours," Brace said, leaning close to my ear.

I loved the way we could alternate between mental speech and speaking out loud with ease. "She was a previous Empress, stepping down after her two hundred years."

I'd only that morning learnt that a ruler only held the crown for two hundred years, unless death took them earlier. They had to then step aside for the next family member, or one born under the blood moon.

Jinissara was the final one to greet Lucas. He actually gave her a half-bow, his head dipping respectfully. She lifted the large, ornate and intricate crown from its resting place, her lips shifting as she spoke. I couldn't hear what was said, but Lucas nodded once and then he again lowered his head. The jewels flashed as the ornate crown clicked into place on top of his gold-leaf wreath. A deep tone chimed out as the bells were struck. The note echoed throughout.

"And so it is complete."

These five words rang out as everyone spoke. Well, everyone who had done this before; most of our group was silent. Lucas turned to face his people and that was some type of signal for the room to be seated again. There were no television shows or anything on First World. Instead, a satellite-type device broadcast important events into the sky; I imagined that everyone around First World would be watching this. I waited to hear Lucas' words.

"I am honored to accept the position of Emperor of First World. A position that is in my blood, a position for which I was groomed and educated." His expression fell a little. He took a deep breath before continuing. "I truly wish my father could be here. The fact that I accept this mantle after his loss is the only sorrow. All bless Emperor Christian."

As he finished, the crowd echoed his words.

"Over the next few weeks I will meet with all the mayoral heads. They will bring forward the concerns from your lands. We never rush to implement change, but I want us to continue to prosper as a race."

He shifted back, his eyes darting to the pillow that rested between the chairs. His head snapped up.

"Aribella, I am going to need you to come up here."

I froze at the sound of my name. My eyes widened as Lucas locked me in his gaze.

"You've got to be freaking kidding me," I muttered.

That sneaky asshat was going to do something stupid, I just knew it.

I didn't move.

"Aribella," he said again.

Every face was turned in my direction. I fought the urge to flip him off.

"Well played, Lucas, you scum bag, well played," Lucy said, loud enough for everyone to hear.

Gasps rang out as I stood; I didn't want a riot to erupt, but I wasn't going up there if I could help it. I wasn't the only one to stand. Brace, Talina, Fury and Lucy followed my movement.

"Calm yourself," Lucas said a huge grin on his face. "I was just going to introduce you to First World, since you've been missing for so long."

"I call bull-shit." This came from Fury.

A pair of guards stepped forward. "You must show Emperor Lucas respect, or you will find yourself locked in the castle holding cell."

Fury looked at me for a moment, before both of us fell about laughing hysterically. I actually had to wipe away tears.

"Do you not know who we are?" Colton, who had been lazing back in his chair, stood now. "We are Walkers, and there isn't a cell on First World which could keep us captive."

He genuinely looked confused as he continued.

"I thought everyone knew about us. I mean, damn, Josian lives on First World."

I interrupted before all-out war erupted. "What do you want, Lucas?"

"I want you to accept your fate." He projected the words loudly. "You were born under the blood moon. You are the daughter of Lallielle, family of Empresses. This is your destiny."

Everyone fell silent as his words were allowed to seep into the air. Brace shifted next to me.

"Don't," I said in a low voice, my hand on his arm. "It's not worth it, and if you kill him I'll have to sit through another stupid Emperor ceremony."

Lucy laughed.

"It is enough that First World can see and acknowledge you," Lucas said. "One day, when your mission is finished, you will have no choice."

The tension broke as the attention shifted from us. I sat again, glaring my displeasure at Lucas. Eventually he was going to understand, or I was going to force him to. At that thought my laluna disappeared from my hand and I had a sneaky suspicion where it was heading.

Lucas paused in the middle of his thank-you speech when a bright light burst around the throne chairs. My laluna had joined with the red royal stone. Their combined purple light shimmered and mesmerized.

"Emperor Lucas has been blessed by the stones," a male voice boomed from the crowd.

"First time in a half a millennium that both stones have been joined," said another, female this time.

Lucas looked shocked at first as the purple light surrounded him. Then his head snapped up and he caught my eye. He knew the blue laluna was mine, and now he was thinking all sorts of impossible things. I could tell.

Dammit, what was that stone up to? Was it the one giving me the weird dreams of First World and its people?

"I will take this as a sign of great things to come for First World." Lucas finally spoke. "And on that note it's time to prepare for the ball."

Noise erupted as everyone began to shift, stand and chat. There was an hour free now for people to get ready for the inauguration dance. Thank the gods I wasn't staying, especially after Lucas' little stunt. Although Lucy was annoyed she couldn't wear the shoes I'd given her for her birthday. But I would rather be venturing to the next world, even with all its possible dangers.

"Are you sure we can't stay for one dance?" Lucy pleaded with me.

I laughed at her woebegone expression. "Uh, count me out, but I'll wait for you back at the house if you want."

She sighed, her shoulders shifting. "Nah, it's okay." Her eyes flicked to Colton. "No one worth dancing with anyways."

I could be wrong but it looked as if Colton's features hardened.

Brace and I exchanged a glance.

Do I need to have a word with Colt?

Brace's words held concern. He loved his friend but Lucy was important to me, so she was important to him.

No, leave it for now. They're managing.

Lucy and I needed to have a serious chat, though. I had no idea how she was really feeling about all of these events. Including her emergence as a soothsayer. We just never had any time for a girl talk. In fact Talina and Fury might also benefit from a big gossip session when we all had five minutes. Therapy for girls. When I got back from the next planet, I was locking it in.

Josian and Lallielle stepped up to us. "So you're heading out to Regali?" Lallielle said, smiling.

"Yeah." I nodded. "No point waiting around. We have to get the fourth girl before the next Seventine is released. Or at least with enough time for the ritual."

"Alright, do you remember where you're supposed to go?" Josian's bronze eyes were flat; something was bothering him. "And who's going with you?"

I reached out and took his hand, sure that he needed comfort. I was learning how Walkers worked, and touch was something that eased their worries. They were very tactile people.

"I remember where to go: the jungle of Artwon. And Lucy, Colt and Brace are coming."

A shadow fell over us. "Greetings, Frayre family and friends. We need to speak of the dark mountains."

We all spun around. Quarn stood there, dressed in the same finery as the royal guards. But maybe decorated with a few more medals and decals. Quarn was a very special and revered man on First World. He had a rare gift – he was a guardian – and his skills were unsurpassed.

"I would like to head across the mountains straight after this dance."

Quarn said the word 'dance' in the same tone as I would say 'bikini wax'. It was clear that he didn't want to be at the ball, but since the castle security was under his control right then, he would never leave during the event.

"Yes, we're ready to go as soon as you are," Lallielle said to her old friend. "Jos will transport everyone across."

"I guess that means we have to go to this dance," Fury said with a sigh, but I could see gleams of hidden excitement in her eyes.

I doubted this was something she'd had a chance to do before. Her planet, Crais, was burning hot, and she had mostly lived underground in the rocks. That harsh life was mainly about survival. Dances fell pretty low on their list of priorities.

Talina took her hand. "Come on, let's go find some dresses. Lalli has outfitted our rooms upstairs with like a million choices."

They moved closer to me and Lucy.

"You two stay safe." Talina hugged us.

"And remember to get us if you need help. We're a team," Fury added.

She didn't hug; that wasn't her style. But I knew she had my back. She was big on the half-Walker girl-power.

"We'll be back before you know it. And you have to be careful in the mountains," Lucy said, her eyes glazing over a bit. "I can't see it. Somehow it's staying just out of sight, but there's something really bad under there."

"And on that uplifting note, we're off." Talina winked at me. "I keep hoping Lucy is just being overdramatic."

We all laughed, and I waved as my friends moved away to take those curving stairs up to the next level where they had a room. Not many people had been able to stay in the castle for this ceremony. Mostly they were set up in the castle grounds. An exception had been made for us.

"Look after my girl," Josian said to Brace. "And get back here soon."

Josian was still acting strange, his tone gruffer than usual.

"I don't need anyone to look after me, Dad. I'm kick-ass all on my own."

He usually laughed at my false arrogance. I had nothing on most Walkers. But this time he just smiled before pulling me in for a hard yet brief hug.

"I love you," he said simply as he pulled away.

My mother's arms replaced his, and then they were gone.

It was the same every time I moved to another planet. Worry, concern and finally resignation from my parents. There was nothing they could do to stop this: it was my quest. This time felt a little worse, though, and it was something to do with Josian. I didn't have time right now, but I would figure it out when I got back.

"Is Josian alright?" Lucy asked. She must have noticed it as well.

I shook my head. "I don't know. Something's bothering him, but he didn't seem ready to share it."

"He's worried," Brace said, his warm hand finding mine.

I felt myself relax.

"The countdown is on, and we aren't getting any closer to stopping the Seventine. He knows that if we don't succeed you'll be facing them in the final battle." His voice hardened. "It's something that has us all a little concerned."

I sucked in a breath and exchanged a glance with Lucy. Imagine if they knew about the vision.

"Alright, let's head to Artwon. I want to check out this jungle. For some reasons Mags says I'll love it there." Colton stretched to his full height. He was about an inch shorter than Brace, which was still giant.

"Has she been many places?" I asked.

"She's been everywhere," he replied.

Lucy opened her mouth.

I shook my head. "No, Lucy."

Her lips started doing that pouting thing she'd perfected. "Come on, he left that so wide open."

Colton narrowed his eyes at her, but I was pretty sure the Walkers had missed the angle Lucy had taken on those words.

We moved out of the main entrance to a small unused alcove. Brace opened a doorway back to the white meeting room at the Angelisian house. It was still a mess from my collision with it earlier, although the window was now covered with a temporary board.

We split up to grab our bags. I don't know why we bothered. We seemed to lose the packs as soon as we got to the planet, and we could open a doorway if things ever got serious. But it was a silly comfort to know you had spare clothes and food.

I was dressed in dark tight fitted jeans. They were a light, stretchy material, and I had them tucked into sturdy, flat black boots. I had on a trim shirt, and a jacket was in my bag. I figured a jungle was going to be hot, but who knew on these planets? It could be anything.

My hair hung loose down my back so I quickly braided it. Time to go.

"You look stunning."

My eyes found him immediately. He was leaning against the wall, his intensity drowning every sense I possessed. I couldn't stop myself from crossing to him.

"I love you," I said, staring up at him.

The liquid chocolate of his eyes softened as he drew me into his arms. His lips came down gently. I fell greedily into the kiss. I needed every single one of these. As always, the heat between us had the kiss deepening, the need exploding and –

"You have to stop or we won't be making it to the jungle," Brace groaned against my mouth. "Which is fine by me."

I laughed, pulling back gently. "You have to stop with this screw-the-world-let's-run-away business. I'm starting to consider it."

"I'm ready when you are."

As he stepped away I noticed his clothes for the first time. He was dressed in his usual army-style cargo pants, dark gray, and a fitted white shirt. The white was the perfect frame for his olive skin tone and dark features. No wonder I couldn't stop kissing this man. He was just far too delicious and perfect, and I was turning into one of those sappy girls.

I shook it off. I needed to focus. Time to get the fourth girl.

Chapter 6

I was trying very hard to breathe, but I was pretty sure there was no air on Regali. Where there should be oxygen it seemed there was water, that's how dense the air was. We'd just stepped free of Colton's doorway into a reasonably clear place in the jungle. This spot was courtesy of Magenta's memory of Regali. I did wonder if she could be trusted not to send us straight into whatever natural dangers existed here. But so far the only thing that looked to be killing us was the moisture in the air.

"If I knew we were going to a sauna, I'd have worn a bikini," Lucy huffed out. "And I'll be the first to say holy eff."

I looked around. "Word. So any ideas how we're going to move through this jungle?"

I felt extremely small and insignificant at that moment. The trees surrounding us were massive, spanning high into the sky. And the canopy was so thick that I couldn't even see the color above. There were smaller plants as well. In fact the entire area looked impenetrable from the round clearing we were standing in. Blue streams of light filtered through the leaves, but it was dim under the canopy.

"Have you ever seen such a beautiful color?" Lucy had moved a little away from us and she was crouched down.

I stepped over behind her to peer over her shoulder. And that's when I saw the sight that had Lucy enthralled.

They were purple open-budded flowers, growing in small, tight bunches around the edge of a tree. The purple was not any old ordinary color. It was light lilac with a pearly sheen streaking the petals.

I had to move closer also. There was something fascinating about the beauty of this plant. I reached out a hand to touch them.

I heard the shouted warning from behind, but it was too late.

Lucy, who was closer, reached them first. Her hand had only just brushed along the stem when the thorns emerged from their hiding place.

"Ouch!" she cried out, withdrawing her hand.

Her cry had been enough for me to halt halfway to the flower. I managed to avoid the large spikes.

"Are you okay?" Colton was beside us. He reached out to take Lucy's limp hand.

"I'm not sure." Her voice wavered. "It doesn't hurt too much, but I feel a little strange."

"We need to move now." Brace's voice was low. "Someone's coming."

"We need to make sure Lucy's okay first," Colton shot back.

And then she fainted. I caught her head before it hit the ground.

"What happened to her?" I bit out.

This couldn't be from shock. The thorns had only left two small punctures.

Brace reached out and, managing to avoid the hidden thorns, snatched one of the flowers from the bunch. He brought it close to his nose.

"It has a scent; it's bitter," he said. "I'm guessing there's poison laced in these thorns."

I couldn't help the gasp which escaped. "What do we do then? We have no idea what the poison is and how to counter it."

Colton reached down and pulled Lucy up into his arms. "We have to find a local. They'll be the only ones with knowledge about what we're dealing with."

Brace placed both hands on my friend's chest, above her heart. He muttered a few words, despite the glare Colton leveled on him.

"I've slowed her heart down, just a little, which will give us more time before the poison spreads."

I stood on tiptoes to give him a hard kiss. "Thank you. Now let's find a Regali native."

"No need to go anywhere," Brace said, "someone's above us right now."

I remembered him saying that before. I glanced up into the canopy. The trees were a multitude of colors, from the standard green to burnt reds, olives, browns and even some black. They looked diverse and dangerous. As if time had not touched this world. But they also looked like they would be great camouflage for anyone hiding.

"Hello," I screamed up. "Please, we need some help; my friend has been hurt."

There was a slight rustling but no one moved into my view.

"Can you see them?" I asked Brace, who was also peering up.

His brow furrowed. "I think I'm seeing something, but I'm not sure it's right."

"Get your ass down here, or I'm coming up and things are going to get very messy." Colton was practically growling. His voice had lowered into a register not usually accessible to humans.

The rustling sounded again, closer than before. I spun once, but there was nothing behind me. Well, nothing I could see. My heart rate sped up. Not only were we facing these unknown Regali inhabitants, but Lucy was still unconscious. And I didn't like the pale nature of her face. She was losing color at a rapid rate.

"Brace, now!" Colton barked the order at him.

And despite the fact he was the new Princeps of Abernath, he obeyed his friend without question or even a glare. I blinked once and Brace was gone. Almost immediately the noises started in earnest around us: screeches, falling debris and this odd thumping beat.

"How is she?" I asked Colton, my words tense.

"Pulse is weak." He wiped at her brow. "She's cold and her skin is leaking fluid."

Typical Walker, unused to the frailties of a normal human body. Cold and sweaty didn't sound like a good combination. I caught a flash of white in the upper trees. It looked like Brace's shirt. Suddenly a large branch was visible over our heads, falling at a rapid rate. Colton was ten times faster than me, shoving me clear and still managing to move and stay on his feet with Lucy.

I landed on my hands and knees about three feet from where I'd stood. The leaves and thin branches had crashed onto my legs and for a moment I was trapped. I struggled and was just about to wiggle free when a thump landed in front of my downturned face. Two objects moved into my vision. I lifted my head slowly, wondering if I was seeing correctly. I was pretty sure the objects were feet, but they weren't human.

"Abby, you have to move now." Colton words blasted through me.

I managed to jag my legs free and rolled to the left as a pair of heavy hands came down near my face.

Hands that matched the feet. They were paws, like those of a large lion, but they were clearly bipedal.

I lifted my head to take in the entire image.

It was furry. A short dense golden-colored fur covering its entire body. It was male – the fur partially concealed it's very obvious male genitalia – but nothing short of pants would fully hide it. I quickly continued up to the face. He was half lion, half humanoid. Such a strange but perfect combination of human and beast. Growls dribbled from his throat. He bared his mouth of razor-sharp teeth at me.

"Wait!" I yelled, sensing he was ready to pounce on me. "We're not your enemy."

The very bright green eyes regarded me for a moment. He was intelligent and fiercely beautiful in a very primitive way. A few more growls emerged. They almost sounded like talking.

I held my hands up in front of me, and when he didn't attack I slowly unfolded my legs and moved into a crouch, then up to standing. All the while my eyes remained locked on the lion-man.

"So I'm going on the assumption that you don't speak English."

With a flicker of his tail – yes, he had a tail – he was suddenly gone.

"Are you okay, Red?" Colton, using Brace's nickname for me, shouted from across the large branch that separated us.

"Fine. How's Lucy?" More importantly.

"She's holding on." He shifted his head, looking around. "Do you know where Brace went?"

I opened our bond.

Brace, you okay, jungle man?

Warm laughter crossed my mind.

I'm a little tied up at the moment. Apparently their queen controls the vines, because they have me wrapped up tight.

I couldn't help the laugh that escaped.

Are you telling me the big bad Princeps of Abernath is tangled in some plants and can't get himself free?

He growled at me.

Gee, everyone wanted to growl at me today.

She has energy power. I could fight her, but then we'd have every inhabitant of this jungle on our asses. That wouldn't be helpful.

He paused for a moment. *And I'm still badass.*

I laughed again, cutting it off at the thump in front of me.

Another lion – I looked down quickly – woman this time – was standing before me. She had a huge mane, much taller around her face than the male one.

"Who are you?"

I sighed in relief. Her words were low and growled, but I managed to understand the rough English.

"We need your help. My friend was pricked by the thorns on your purple flowers." I spoke slowly, pointing down to the many plants which lined the path.

"You speak tongue of the gods." Her gray-green eyes flicked to her left.

Colton was moving toward us. Lucy was deathly pale. If I hadn't been able to hear the faint thump-thump of her heartbeat I would have suspected we were too late.

"I am Klea, a leon and royal guard."

The lion-woman – Klea – drew my attention again.

"Only our Queen can help your friend, but I do not trust you."

"Klea, always with the overprotecting. You know I am safe." Lyrical words rang out from the large bushes around us.

I watched in amazement as the greenery parted and out stepped the most stunningly beautiful woman I'd ever seen. She was taller than I was, her skin a tawny golden color. Her hair looked like it almost reached her calves, a silky brown in a shade darker than her skin, with green ivy patterns spanning all the way.

And the eyes – unbelievable. They were violet-colored, shaped into an exotic slant. She was dressed in a two-piece outfit that I was pretty sure was a patchwork of leather and plant.

When she stepped free of the plants, she looked like she was gliding across the mossy ground, her bare feet treading gently.

"Place her on the ground." The Queen's musical voice echoed again.

She stopped at Colton's side, Klea moving in to stand protectively at her back.

Colton crouched to gently lay Lucy on the soft green ground covering. The woman reached behind to carefully pluck up a purple flower.

She leaned her head over it. "Thank you for your sacrifice," she murmured.

I hovered closer as she opened Lucy's pale lips. Then she tilted the flower and a few drops of liquid fell from the center of the bud into my friend's mouth.

"This calia flower holds the power of death and life. Very few would think that which poisons could also save," the Queen said.

Lucy started to cough. She wrinkled her nose and I gasped as pink flooded back into her features. It was as if she'd been a wax statue suddenly brought to life.

"Your friend will be fine." The Queen regarded me solemnly, her eyes roaming my features. "I am Ria. I must say I am surprised to find strangers in my jungle. Why have you come?"

I opened my mouth to answer, but slammed it shut again as a bunch of vines dropped down in front of me. From the center emerged a black-eyed but still semi-smiling Brace.

"Sorry about that. You were too strong to fight. I only wanted to calm you down," Ria addressed him. Her tone of voice was so soothing; everything about her exuded tranquility.

"No problem," he said shortly.

I could tell he understood and was fine with what had happened in the trees.

"Are you okay?" Colton's soft words had me spinning my head back to Lucy.

Her eyes were open. She was staring up into his face.

"Why am I on the ground?" she asked. "What happened?"

"Don't touch the purple flowers," I said with a grin.

Now that she was okay, things felt much more relaxed.

"They're a lot like you: pretty on the outside and deadly under the petals."

She laughed as she struggled up to a sitting position. Colton moved back then, some of the warmth and concern he'd displayed disappearing. Ria was the one to help Lucy to her feet.

"Holy hotness," Lucy said as she looked between me and the Queen. "Usually, Abbs, I think you're the most beautiful woman I've ever seen, but she might have you beat."

I nodded. "Oh, yeah, she's kicking my butt in the hot scale." I could admit it; no use denying the truth.

"Not even close," Brace muttered.

I smiled at my loyal mate.

"So who are you and where do I get eyes like that?" Lucy grinned at her savior.

"I am Ria, Queen of the beasts. I rule the jungle of Artwon, which is a small country of Regali."

She paused. "And I inherited these eyes from my father."

"Damn." Lucy smiled even bigger. "I just want to follow her around like a puppy."

She looked at Colton. "You must be struggling; try not to hump her leg."

He opened his mouth to reply but was cut off.

"Why do you speak in the tongue of the gods?" Klea, the leon, growled at us from where she stood rigidly looming over Ria. "Our Queen is born of god and mother-to-nature. You speak in their language."

"Actually, this language originates with Walkers. They've spread it throughout the worlds during their constant travels." Brace moved in to stand at my back, his warmth and presence encasing me.

"Walkers." Ria sounded startled. "What do you know of Walkers? Is that why you wear the marks? I thought they were purple."

Okay, definitely not the first time she'd heard of Walkers.

"That's why the color of your eyes is so familiar," Colton said. "It's almost identical to the color of Nos' eyes."

"Indigo," I breathed. "Yes, you're my half-Walker."

Great, she was the Queen. Should be easy to get her to leave.

Hours later we were up in her tree-house. Apparently Magenta had sent us straight to beneath her royal dwelling, probably hoping we'd be attacked by her guards. During our time on Regali so far I'd explained the important facts to Ria: my mission to gather the half-Walkers, the Seventine release, and finally how important it was that we attempted the ritual which would hopefully suck the freed back in and permanently seal the doorway. Ria had listened, asked questions that did more than hint at the cunningly intelligent mind she possessed. But in the end we'd reached an impasse.

"I am Queen. There is none to take over my duties, and I cannot just abandon my people," she said for the third time. "And while I appreciate what you are saying is universal, what would be the point of saving Regali if Artwon and its inhabitants are lost during my absence?"

"Who would rule if you died?" I asked.

She faced me. Her almond-shaped eyes blinked a few times in rapid succession. "If I died, normal protocol would be followed. We have rules and rituals in place for this. We have no precedent for a ruler to simply create a hiatus." She smiled. "No matter how important the issue."

"Besides, we have nothing but your word. Why should we believe this tale you weave?" Klea growled, which I was beginning to understand was just the way she spoke.

The beasts, as Ria called them, didn't have vocal cords suitable for speaking English.

"I believe them," Ria said simply.

I was totally digging how chilled out and confident she was.

"They speak of my father's words and they know his name."

I reached for my necklace then and flicked the clasp. Brace and I wore permanent marks, but as the yellow light emerged, so did Colton's black tribal and Ria's indigo pattern.

Klea stopped her growling and pacing, and just stared at her Queen. And I couldn't blame her. The indigo pattern matched the purple tones of Ria's eyes. She looked even more stunning. I glanced around but there was nothing reflective in the simple tree-house.

"Go to the lake, Ria. You need to see your face," Klea said to her.

"Wait," I said, before reluctantly handing over my world necklace. I never usually let it out of my sight. "You will need the moonstale light."

She disappeared out of the open doorway. It looked as if she just stepped off into nothing, and we were very high up. But then I noticed the vines catch her, lowering her to the ground.

"Coolest power ever," Lucy said.

I reached out an arm and hugged my tiny friend. "I'm so glad you're okay." It had been a close call.

"I feel fantastic," she said. "Remind me to take those flowers with me when I leave."

"Don't let them hear you say that. They take offense to murder." Ria reappeared behind us.

Her tone was light, but there was truth behind those words.

"Are the plants sentient here?" I asked.

"Plants are sentient everywhere. You just have to learn to listen." She ran her hands over the ivy blocking the doorway. "But I have special abilities courtesy of my mother. She is one of the tree spirits. I am her only child." Her eyes dulled as she spoke. "She doesn't exist on this plane anymore. We communicate via the sacred tree only."

"I'm guessing that you're going to be one of the more powerful half-Walkers." Brace was leaning against one of the only solid walls. "You're not only Walker, but the other half is a nature spirit."

"Don't you see?" I implored her. "We need you; we need your energy. This might be our only chance."

She gave Klea a quick glance, before turning back to me. "I wish I could leave. But we have many dramas in Artwon right now. The fringe are back, and I have discovered that they are not only gathering factions of Regali, but they also work with Walkers. Together they plan to bring about the destruction of all packs."

"What's the fringe?" I asked.

"They are those of our packs who have rebelled. They do not like the way Ria lives: in peace. Ria has almost wiped out warring between our people. The fringe like to war," Klea answered.

"How do you know Walkers assist them?" Brace moved to stand at my side.

"My father, Nos, came and showed me how they hid from my plants. While we were there, we saw men emerge from a black starry doorway. My father identified them as Walkers."

"How many," Brace spoke again, "and what was their clan?"

"Only two," she replied, "and I believe it was Abanaith. Or something like that."

Brace's features darkened. Quite a few of the Abernath clan were loyal to Que, his recently departed father, and Brace was having difficulty rounding them up and halting their activities around the worlds.

"If we help you with your problem, would you consider leaving?" I knew it could be time-consuming, but I needed Ria.

She pursed her lips. "I do not know if what you ask is possible. But, if the fringe are not exterminated then it would be *impossible* for me to leave."

So she was promising nothing.

"Alright, then let's get on our fringe-busting outfits and go do some pest-spraying." Lucy jumped to her feet, her eyes bright, curls bouncing everywhere. She looked like the picture of health.

Of course Klea and Ria had no idea what Lucy had just said, but they joined the rest of us on our feet.

"First, we call a meeting of all the pack guards," Ria said. "And then we go in with as much force as we can gather and take them down. Either they surrender or they die." Her words were harsh, but her tone was still chilled out.

Kind of freaky, the way she so calmly discussed death.

"And I'll deal with the Walkers," Brace finished.

Ria led us through the jungle. The plants simply parted for her as she walked. I couldn't even imagine having that kind of power over nature.

And it wasn't just that. As she walked, she touched each plant and they curled around her. There was some type of love-love relationship going on there. No wonder humans were drawn to her. Her aura was so warm and inviting. All shades of yellow. After walking for a long time in the sauna of a jungle, we finally reached a reasonably large clearing.

"This is the center of the packs' territories." Ria sank onto the ground. "Please avoid that vine." She pointed to a large mass of vines with small black berries. "It is a little temperamental."

Remembering the calia flowers, we moved as far from those brambles as we could before sitting in a semi-circle.

"So how many different packs are there in Artwon?" Lucy asked, leaning forward to rest her elbows on her knees.

"There are six. The leons." Ria smiled at Klea. "The small cat people are the jags." As she said this a pair of black-furred creatures swung into the clearing. They did look like cats with short coarse fur, whiskers and pointed ears.

"The eaglets, flyers."

In they came, from high in the canopy. They were the strangest combination I'd seen so far. Standing as tall as a man, they had wings and arms. Their finger-tips had razor-sharp claws, and a mass of feathers coated their bodies. All the while with a human face ... well, a human face topped off with a beak.

"The slimes are the reptiles."

I pulled my eyes from the eaglets to see the slimes. They emerged from the bushes around us, and I had to suppress my shivers. They were built like snakes, with long slimy bodies that looked to be scaled, but they had human-shaped heads, and claw-like arms and legs. A long forked tongue emerged as they looked us over.

"The munks are our tree flyers," Ria continued.

Their cooing noises preceded them as they swung in. They were monkey-like creatures ... no, not really monkey. More like an ape and human had merged with each other. Short dark fur coated their bodies, which were the closest in shape to human.

"And our most ferocious, the bera."

I almost got to my feet as the seven-foot-tall bera entered our clearing. They were the epitome of a grizzly bear, but with a humanoid face. Not many things I'd seen topped out Walkers in height and strength, but there was something scary about the bera.

"This is the strangest thing I've ever seen," Lucy whispered to me.

The members of the different packs started to move closer to us to join in sitting around the semi-circle. I couldn't take my eyes off them, searching out each individual feature. Suddenly one of the jags let out a loud screech. I winced as its brethren followed its noise, and suddenly they surrounded Colton.

Ria stood. "You're a wolver?" There was a question in her voice as she faced him.

He slowly stood also, his aim clearly not to startle the jags, who were closing in on him.

"What's a wolver?" he asked.

"They were a pack who warred themselves to death. We have not seen them in many years."

"I'm a Walker," Colton said, his pale blue eyes flashing in warning as the black cats closed in. "I've never been to Regali in my life. But I do shift into a wolf, a canine animal."

"Yeah, a dog, like woof-woof, you know?" Lucy piped up.

She was still teasing Colton, but I could see her moving closer and getting her hands up to defend him.

"No, not like a dog. I'm a wolf. Completely different," Colton said as he stepped in front of her, edging her out of the jags' sight.

Ria turned and spoke in growls to the small cat people. They stopped the screeching and started to calm down.

Klea was at her Queen's back. "I thought you smelt familiar when we first met. It is similar to the wolver, but there are many subtle differences. The jags probably missed this. Their sense of smell is not quite as developed as the leons'," she said as she grabbed one of the jags by the scruff of the neck and threw it backwards.

Then she growled what sounded like harsh warnings, and all of the rest moved away.

Once the packs had calmed down and taken their seats, Ria moved into the center of the clearing.

"I have found the fringe." She projected her voice out into the clearing and silence descended faster than you could blink an eye. "I know we have been waiting for this moment for a long time and finally I know how they have managed to avoid capture and stay undetected."

Growls, screeches, chirps, cheeps and many other noises rang out in a chorus of song. Or speech. I couldn't tell.

"I need to prepare you all, though. They wear the skins of our dead." Ria choked out these words. "They use the pure essence of our loved ones to hide their evil ways."

I was sure that tears rolled down the faces of almost all of the animal-people in our midst, although it was hard to gauge expressions on their furred, scaled and feathered features. Sorrow rose in an engulfing emotion and I found a few stray tears rolling down my own cheeks at this outpouring of pain.

Brace reached up and, with both hands resting on my face, he used his thumbs to brush away the salty wetness. He gave me a gentle kiss on the lips for comfort, nothing more. I stared at him, unable to pull my eyes away until Ria broke the sorrowful silence.

"We will leave in a few moments. The rest of the guards are on their way, and none should miss this moment." Ria lifted both hands skywards.

The vines from up in the canopy dropped down.

"Are you okay to travel on the vines?" she asked us.

"No problem," Lucy said without hesitation.

"Hold up," I said. "What does that mean?"

"The vines will swing us through the jungle. It is the fastest way to travel through the canopy."

Sounded insanely unsafe to me, but hey, six months before who would have thought I'd walk through a wall into First World, let alone everything else that had happened since.

"Let's do this." I jumped to my feet.

We'd left our packs at Ria's place, so all I had were my sweaty clothes, and myself. And that was all I needed.

Chapter 7

I couldn't find the right words to describe our journey through the trees. Once my initial fear faded – being thrust at a breakneck pace toward branches, trees and vines – I couldn't help but enjoy every moment. The speed, the scent of the forest, which was earthy but with sweet flowery aromas intermingling, and the freedom of flying.

We were surrounded on all sides by the different pack members. Some of them flew; some jumped through the branches; and others also used the vines.

The forest was too densely packed for us to be able to do this without Ria parting the branches. It was a once in a lifetime experience. I was having a lot of those lately.

All too soon our momentum slowed, and I gave a final sigh as my vines lowered me down. Ria said she would get everyone as close as possible; we would be downwind to hide our scent, but we still had to stay quiet. On the ground I hugged close to the base of a massive redwood tree and waited for everyone else to join me.

Brace's arms encircled me from behind.

I've done a lot of things in my life. But that was definitely fun. He sounded happy.

I tilted my head back so he could lean down and gently lay a kiss on my lips. We pulled apart as Ria, followed by Lucy and Colton, crept out of the bushes to our right.

"The rest of the packs are around us in the trees." Ria's words were so low I barely caught them. "There was no activity in the fringe entrance just before, so follow me and we will hit them hard and fast."

I gathered energy, keeping it close to the palm of my right hand. Josian had been teaching me how to load my arm up like a gun, saving precious seconds when I needed them.

"Let me go first," Brace murmured. "I'll clear the initial path."

With a nod Ria made sure Brace stayed close to her. She waved toward a large leafy overhang that was bordered on one side by a waterfall. On the other was a massive ravine. There was only one entrance, under the overhang.

It was the perfect camouflage from anyone looking down from the canopy. You would be able to see nothing but overhanging leaves framed by two natural wonders. Although, unless I was mistaken, there seemed to be animal furs hung in the branches of the trees surrounding the area.

"Under the canopy," Ria murmured.

Brace shifted around her. I could feel him gather energy. Our powers were connected with each other, but his energy dominated mine. The buildup sent shivers along my skin. The hairs stood up on my arms.

Could everyone feel the powerful storm he was about to release?

It felt as if the jungle knew. The leaves around us turned inward, moving toward the source of power.

My mate took two large steps and, with both hands thrust forward, he released his energy. The leaves ruffled on the fern-like plant, but I knew the real burst would come in the underground lair.

He held his hand up for one moment, halting our shifting.

"Okay," he finally spoke, "we can go now."

Klea let out a rumble, which was quiet, but seemed to echo through the trees, ricocheting from one large branch to the next, and before I knew it the rumbling sound filled the space.

All of us moved as one – and we weren't alone. The pack guards came in from all sides to join us. I ducked my head as we hit the entrance, although leaves still brushed along my curls. The sensation was wet and unpleasant.

Under the canopy was a large tunnel opening. My eyes adjusted as we moved into the initial darkness, but there was light just ahead. The space wasn't really underground. Instead it moved along the edge of the waterfall, and we emerged on the other side into a large space hidden behind the falling water.

"So clever," Ria said, "the thunder-falls hide their activities. They have plenty of food and water here. It is the perfect place to set up a base."

The space wasn't empty. Brace's energy had knocked down the ones who must have been closest to the entrance. I noticed that the fallen fringe were mainly bera, and I was glad to not be facing these seven-foot enemies straight up. Although there were a few bodies that didn't look like pack.

I stepped around three small ones, squinting as I looked closer. They reminded me of garden gnomes with bulbous noses and rosy cheeks, and they'd be cute if they didn't have that creepy gremlin feel to them.

Next to them was a stick insect in man form, about the size of a large rabbit, and lastly something that resembled a boulder with eyes and short arms and legs.

"What's that smell?" Lucy asked, wrinkling her nose.

"Blood," Brace said shortly.

"Yes," Colton agreed, "much blood has been spilled in this area."

"This is where they skin our dead," Ria bit out.

She pointed her hand across to the wall and as I turned to examine the macabre scene a coughing gasp fell from my lips. Was there a way to scrub one's mind? Because I really needed to unsee everything about this scene.

There were two carcasses suspended upside down against the back wall. One was a munk and the other a jag. There were round wooden bowls beneath them to catch the blood as it dripped down.

Beside them were two more, but I couldn't tell what they had been because they no longer had their skin. Instead they were just bloody masses of muscle, organ and bone.

And behind them there were literally hundreds of skins spread out in various stages of drying.

"I do not care any longer about offering them a chance to surrender. They all die," Ria said, her voice as sharp as broken glass.

The howls and shrieks that accompanied her words indicated the packs agreed.

And I totally understood.

This was a horrific thing to see, and if any of my family members had been strung up like that ... Well, I'm not sure how I would have reacted.

The guards swiftly dealt with the fringe who'd been knocked unconscious. Let me tell you, their teeth and claws were as sharp and lethal as they looked. I turned my head at the last moment, right before the heads were severed.

No matter how much I immersed myself in this life, and how much battle and carnage we caused, I was never going to be comfortable with death. There was too much Earth human in me. We're raised to fear death. Humans have short, often volatile lives, and they live knowing they may not be there the next day. I guess it's the same for all worlds, but some races are harder to kill than others.

"Twenty dead, Queen, which is but a fraction of their numbers." Klea strode over to where we stood.

We were close to the entrance. I stood as far from the dead and as close to the fresh air as I could.

"Let's find the rest," Ria said. For the first time there was no warmth in her voice.

"Just like mother nature," Lucy whispered to me. "One minute she's all warm and sunshine, the next a lightning bolt hits you in the ass."

I stifled my laughter. Perfect analogy to describe Ria.

Once we moved from the waterfall, the cavern darkened. There was one path that led away. Assuming that this was where the fringe had disappeared, we started to move through.

I was drifting along with everyone else, but I was almost against the left wall, my arm scraping the solid black dirt-like material.

Then at some point in our journey I was nudged hard enough to solidly stumble into the wall. I expected a hard thud, but instead of slamming into rock I ended up tumbling straight through the wall into the other side.

I gasped as I finally found my footing and looked around. I was in another tunnel, which I expected ran parallel to where I'd just been.

And I was alone.

I couldn't hear anything, and pushing against the wall resulted in nothing. It must have been one-way. With an audible swallow I turned to face the darkness.

"You're okay, Abby, there's nothing hiding here in the dark." I spoke to myself, deciding it was better to be crazy than pee myself in fear.

I released a small energy ball of light. It hovered near my face. The tunnel was low and narrow, the air stuffy, and for the first time in ages my claustrophobia started to react.

"Don't think about it," I muttered as I crept forward. "There's nothing in here with you and the dirt isn't going to cave in on your head."

I was too panicked to even think about tracing out of there. I couldn't focus long enough to find a tether.

Re ... Red ... hear me.

I stopped as flickers of Brace's voice sounded in my head.

Hello? Brace, I'm in a tunnel next to yours.

My words sounded a little frantic. Why was I so scared right then? There was no reply from Brace.

"You shouldn't have left your friends."

The words echoed around me, and yes, if I'm honest, a small shriek escaped as something brushed my arm.

I spun around, the light drifting with me, but I could see nobody. Who had spoken?

134

"I've been waiting for you, my precious little half."

Bile rose in my throat. No way. Was that the Seventine?

There was nothing around me but the echoing of the ghostly words. I almost hit the ceiling when something brushed me again. I made myself repeat the words that the Walkers had said at the gathering. The Seventine couldn't do anything physical in their current state. They couldn't really do anything to hurt me until they were all released. I must have spoken the words out loud as well, because it answered me.

"The Walkers don't know everything. I have plenty of power. No one truly remembers the originals."

I started to run then.

I didn't care what was ahead of me. I couldn't stay there by myself with the Seventine taunting me. My heart raced. I couldn't remember being that afraid in a long time. Echoing laughter followed me.

I screamed as something grabbed me from the shadows.

At the speed I was racing I couldn't believe anything could have plucked me out of thin air like that. Without hesitation I flung out my arms and legs, and they landed on something very solid. This was not a Seventine; this was something else.

Growls started, and by the time I remembered my light it had swung around to highlight a monster.

Okay, maybe a monster was an exaggeration, but it was freaking scary.

It held me in its large claws. I could feel the tips cutting into my biceps. Its snarling snout was close to my face.

I threw my head back as it snapped once. No doubt those sharp teeth would have severed my throat if I hadn't moved.

Its snout was coming at me again, so I released my previously loaded blast of energy and found myself flung to the ground. I jumped to my feet, ignoring the pain.

This animal was fast. It didn't hesitate to come straight back at me.

Seeing it in the light again, I realized it had definite wolf-like characteristics, but with less human mixed in with the animal – the other packs on Regali seemed to be almost half and half – but it was also not a full wolf either. It had an extended snout, but shorter than an Earth wolf. And the yellow eyes definitely shone with intelligence.

I continued to back away and turn in a circle, never taking my eyes off it. It growled at me. I knew it was communicating, but I didn't speak wolf. Where was Colton when I needed him?

"I am not your enemy." I held up a hand.

Maybe my words would stop this creature like it had the leon when we arrived.

Nope, I couldn't have been more wrong.

The moment the words left my tongue its snarls increased and it leapt at me again. I threw my head back, avoiding the jaws again, but it changed course at the last second and its razor-sharp teeth bit straight into my right shoulder.

I gritted my teeth, whimpers falling from my lips in short, shrill cries. It wasn't letting go and, considering it stood over six feet on its hind legs and was powerfully strong, I didn't know how to free myself. My right arm hung uselessly at my side. I knew that could only mean that the tendon and nerves had been severed.

Using my left hand, I clawed at its eyes. My stomach rolled as my index finger squished into the soft wet socket, but it was about survival now.

It howled, and the lock of its jaw lessened, so I dug deeper. It flung me away, its long tongue darting out to lick at its wounds.

Then it faced me.

One eye was useless and empty, but the other was conveying the fact it was pretty pissed off. My blood coated the lower half of its face and flecked its fur. I noticed something that I'd seen on the other fringe members but hadn't really registered. There was red speckles throughout their fur and, like this freak, it looked like blood. Old, dried crusty blood.

I pulled myself to my feet, right arm still useless and my blood raining down. I almost fell as blood mixed with dirt and rock to create a slippery mess. The pain was a dull register, just sitting behind the adrenalin. I knew I was going to feel it soon, but right then it was time to survive. The creature was blocking the path forward. The only other way was back to the Seventine. And I didn't know which was worse.

While I was trying to decide what to do, it caught me by surprise. This time it latched onto my calf.

I knew what it was doing: systematically cutting off my ability to escape.

By that stage I was down to one functioning arm and leg.

With my last iota of energy, I pictured Ria's loft house and grabbed onto the largest of the shining tethers.

I was jerked through, but in my panic and haste I had forgotten one important factor. Anything touching me was going to come also.

Red.

The roar came through our bond loud and clear this time. Whatever had been blocking us was gone.

Help.

The blood loss was getting to me. I knew what was happening and if I couldn't get away soon I'd probably black out, and then this creature would rip out my throat.

The creature was wrenched away from me and it dropped me again. A large thump sounded in front of me. I lifted my head to find one of the guards: Klea, her golden fur shining in the light from the open doorway.

"Wolver," she growled. "What are you doing here?"

So this was the infamous wolver. No wonder they'd been so ferocious with Colton. Wolvers were not nice puppies.

In my dazed state I struggled to track their fight. But it was clear that Klea had incredible skills. She sprang around the open tree loft with speed and agility. With one eye gone, the wolver had no chance of keeping up. It took her seconds to land on its back. She brought both clawed hands down and with a ripping motion severed its head.

I levered myself up on my good arm. Pain and tingles were replacing the numbness in my right, so it was starting to heal.

"What the Fu –" Brace's roar was interrupted by Klea eviscerating the wolver right in front of me. The dark red of its blood landed in splatters around me.

"Red." Brace lifted me up, supporting my weight with ease. "Baby, are you okay?"

I raised my head, ready with a reassuring smile. Black eyes dominated his face and fear creased his features. He'd been afraid for me.

"I couldn't feel you, I couldn't contact you. What the hell happened?" He was yelling and pulling me closer.

"Can't breathe," I managed to gasp out. I didn't care, though.

"Shit, sorry, I'm probably hurting you." He pulled back far enough to assess my injuries.

His hands brushed gently over my arms. In their wake warmth descended, and I knew he was using his energy to help the healing. His features tightened as he reached my collar bone, but he said nothing until he was finished.

"You okay?" Klea crouched down, her feline features examining me.

I nodded. "Thank you, how did you get here so quickly?"

"When you went missing Ria sent me back here in case you returned to her home. I will let her know you are safe." She howled once into the air and it was in that moment I noticed that it was starting to darken under the canopy. Night was falling. "I need to get back to her," she finished.

"Wait." I stopped her before she leapt from the platform. "I can take you back instantly."

Brace never questioned my decision. He just helped me up. I loved that he was protective without stifling my independence. Mates were definitely designed to complement one another. I grabbed a shirt from my bag to replace my old one, which had been torn to shreds. I turned to the leon.

Klea regarded me with suspicion, but eventually laid her paw into my out-held palm. I curled my fingers around, gripping into the soft fur, thankful that her claws were sheathed. Brace held my other hand.

"Hold on," I said.

Closing my eyes, I mentally pictured the room behind the waterfall. Avoiding any tether in close proximity to the wall of death, I grabbed a glittering strand.

We were there in an instant.

Klea pulled her paw back, looking around with huge eyes. For the first time she looked surprised, but that didn't stop her from shaking out her large mane and bounding along the path we had taken earlier. I got the feeling she didn't like to leave Ria alone for long.

141

"What happened?" Brace questioned me as we followed at a rapid run.

"Got knocked into the wall and this weird trapdoor spun me into another tunnel. I thought I was alone in there, but I kept hearing someone speaking." My voice faltered a little. "I think it was the Seventine."

Brace growled. "That's about the only explanation for why there was a breakdown in our communications. Melding bonds are strong. I didn't know what to think when I couldn't find you. I was getting mental flashes of your panic, but nothing else."

"Yes, well I took off to try and get away from the voice and that wolver took me out." I winced, remembering. "Took me out in the worst kind of way."

Brace reached out and captured my hand as we continued to follow Klea down the path.

"I'm glad Klea was already in the tree-house. I opened a doorway as soon as I felt you, but I might have been too late."

I squeezed his palm. "You can't always save me, Brace. Sometimes I'll save myself, sometimes others will save me and sometimes I'll be the one doing the saving. You have to learn to share the responsibility."

He laughed. "Red, you're now and always my responsibility. I'll always be the one to save you. I'll always come for you. Nothing will stop me." He managed to land a kiss on my lips, even at the speed we were traveling. "You've given me everything, just by existing. So you've done your part for the rest of our lives, now it's my turn."

His words created an unusual feeling inside my chest. Like this weird, warm, heart-flipping-over thing.

"Well, I love you, you crazy control freak," I teased.

He laughed. "I love you, despite the fact you're a pain in my ass."

"That has to be Abbs. I can feel the sappy romance coming down the tunnel."

Lucy's words echoed toward us.

I couldn't help the smile that crossed my lips. I'd probably think we were a bit hard to handle too if I had to see it every day. But when you're in love, you're in love. Not much you can do about it. The need I felt to be with Brace was never going to end.

I bit back the pain of Lucy's vision and the chance I was going to lose Brace. Ironically enough, it was his love that gave me the strength to know I could sever the bond to save everyone. If it came to that.

I could see that we were fast approaching the rest of our group. They were waiting at this weird junction. We slowed when we reached them.

Ria moved out of the shadows and strode toward us, her stunning features creased in concern.

"Klea told me it was a wolver." She laid a warm hand on my arm. "You're lucky. They were the most vicious of any pack. They either warred themselves to death or disappeared many years ago." Her voice hardened. "Apparently some of them survived. I should have known they would be amongst the fringe leaders."

"Did you find any others?" I asked.

"No, we waited here to make sure you were safe." She smiled at me. "After all, you're my Walker sister."

I could tell that she meant those words; they were not empty platitudes. I loved the bond that seemed to exist between us half-Walkers, and wondered if there would be one who would reject us.

"I'm fine, let's keep going." My injuries were mostly healed.

I was tense, though. Dark tunnels were not the best place to be when you'd just been jumped from the shadows.

"Don't you worry, Red girl," Colton said as he sidled closer, "any more wolves appear and I'll rip their throats out for you."

Lucy snorted, interrupting him. "Wow, you say the sweetest things, Colton."

"There's nothing sweet about me, darlin'."

And all of a sudden he had a weird drawling accent.

"I haven't forgotten." Her words were a mutter.

We were moving along the channel now. The packs were out in front, and we were at the back. Ria moved between the two of us with the ever present Klea keeping pace with her.

"There's a mass of energy ahead," Brace said.

As soon as he mentioned it I noticed something odd. I often had strange feelings I ignored, even on Earth, but I was starting to see that there were explanations for some of them. This was a tingling sensation low in my stomach, and I recognized it as foreign energy starting to infiltrate my own. My own energy was always moving, curious and hungry, an endless pit inside that definitely liked to absorb free energy. It was always on the lookout for power. And, as Brace said, we were coming up to a large mass.

"I'll send out my blast again," Brace said as our group rounded the corner. "Wait for me."

But it was too late.

The packs that were ahead of us didn't hear his call, and as soon as they saw the fringe members they charged forward; they were out for blood. We had to increase our speed to keep them in sight. I felt more than saw the battle ahead of us. And we were severely outnumbered. There were at least a hundred of the fringe. They looked to be a mix of the present packs, wolvers and those three other species that had been back behind the waterfall.

The wolvers were the only beasts to be on all fours. They were definitely the least human of any of them. They just looked like massive horse-size wolves, with small amounts of human skin around their eyes. Ria's pack guards had paused about twenty yards from the fringe. The sheer numbers we faced had halted our group.

"The wolvers are shifted like on a red moon," Ria said.

"What do you mean?" Colton asked.

"Once in a forty cycle we have a blood red moon. It calls the packs and they shift into their true animal forms."

"And when the sun comes out they shift back?" Lucy said, her eyes wide with a curious sparkle.

"What is a sun?" Ria asked.

We all stopped what we were doing and stared at her.

"A bright, hot star that brings life to plants and such," I said, trying to remember if I'd seen a sun.

The canopy was so close together, I was pretty sure I'd never even seen the sky.

"We have six moons that cast the blue light of life and the red moon when it appears," Ria said simply. "Is it that to which you refer?"

I shook my head.

"How is it so warm here without a sun?" Lucy asked.

"It is always warm in Artwon. The moons are warm and the jungle holds in the heat."

Well, that was interesting, and did explain the blue tinge. I had thought that was simply the shadows from the canopy. Growls distracted me then. I'd almost forgotten we were facing a wall of crazy fringe members.

"So what do we do now?" I asked. "We're vastly outnumbered."

"We can take care of some of them and even up the numbers," Colton said with a nod toward Brace.

Ria smiled, her flawless teeth flashing in the semi-darkness of this underground hole. The boys took that as an affirmation, stepping forward to the front of our group. I grabbed Lucy's hand and we huddled together to watch as Colton and Brace moved dangerously close to the growling, snarling group.

They stepped quickly in a synchronized series of movements, arms flying outwards, upwards and then forward, and at that moment a shimmery yellow light blasted free from their palms.

I could see the force and if that wall was coming at me I would be running for dear life. But either the fringe were stupid or had no idea how much that energy wall was going to hurt when it hit them, because they didn't shift even a minute amount. At the last minute, before the energy hit, two men stepped forward from the fringe and released their own burst of power.

The two energies collided in midair and the ricocheting force shot everyone back on both sides. I prevented myself and Lucy from hitting the floor by absorbing the power and sucking down the excess energy. But we were only some of the few not to be knocked down. Brace met my eyes across the fallen packs.

"Walkers," he said.

"Stay here," I told Lucy, expecting she would pay no attention to me and, sure enough, she was on my butt as I moved through the masses to reach Brace and Colton.

"Are they of your clan?" I asked him straight away. I was gathering energy, prepared to help any way I could. "And what are we going to do?"

"Zeleath and Arian. Most definitely Abernaths," he said. "And we're going to scatter them throughout the universe."

Colton let out a satisfied snort. "Damn, I love it when bad Brace comes out to play. Just like old times."

And with those words they both disappeared from sight.

Chapter 8

I would have thought, being Walker, I could track their movements, but unless that flash of white was Brace's shirt then I saw nothing. The fringe Abernaths were looking worried now, despite the mass of snarling creatures at their back. Could they feel what was coming at them in the darkness?

The taller of the two, with his lank dishwater brown hair, was looking up into the rock ceiling when he disappeared. His screams echoed around the area, and then were eerily cut off mid-yell. Unease was spreading through the fringe and their last Walker looked nervous.

"Something tells me I should be glad your men are the good Walkers." Ria smiled at me.

"I'm not sure any Walkers can be classified as good." I smiled back.

"And the blond isn't mine, unless you mean as a snarky watchdog," Lucy finished.

Ria looked between us for a moment but didn't make any further comment. I wasn't sure she knew quite how to take us. Pretty typical reaction. We grew on you, like a fungus.

When the echoes of the screams around the rock ceiling finally died out, it felt as if the room held its breath waiting for the next move. But the remaining Walker was having none of that.

"Attack them!" he yelled. "They will kill you otherwise. Don't give them the advantage."

The packs didn't hesitate. As one they moved.

I gathered my energy before letting it go in a large unbroken force. It was the sort of mass power that had burst from me before, but this time I controlled it.

It slammed into the front line, knocking them down, and they thankfully took out a lot of those right behind them. But even with this there were still plenty coming at us. The first of the fringe hit the pack guards. I winced at the snarls, tearing of flesh and blood that followed.

Those fighting blocked the way for the rest of us; everyone pushed forward. Suddenly I was distracted by a whirlwind starting behind the fringe.

The top of the turret was visible over the heads of the bera. It was a massive portal and I could feel it drawing the energy from those closest to it. The fringe members were starting to drift back into its powerful arms, and there was nothing they could do to fight against it. And then just when the majority of their members were at the junction, the energy reversed its direction and instead of sucking in it forced a blast outward. The fringe in its path were destroyed, literally ripped limb from limb.

"I told you that you didn't want to see Brace in his true form." Colton stood at Lucy's side.

He'd been on the other side of the room, but had used his instant transmission to reach us.

My jaw fell open, and I swung back around to observe the crazy tornado more closely. Was Colton saying that Brace was the storm? That would explain why the burst of wind seemed to be directed toward the fringe only. Our packs had backed up, but we were untouched so far.

"Did you know he could do that?" Lucy asked me. "He's a freaking tropical storm."

I shook my head, my eyes wide. "He mentioned that he had some powers he didn't use a lot, but I never expected it was anything like this."

Brace had literally turned into a whirlwind and the power it generated had my teeth aching it was so strong.

"Why doesn't he use that all the time?" I asked.

"He believes that it's something he could lose control of," Colton replied.

"So why now?" Lucy said.

"I'm guessing he's still a little pissed off about Red here disappearing and getting chewed on by a psycho wolver." Colton grinned.

I was thinking he might be right.

By the time Brace had stopped spinning and once again looked like his usual six and a half feet of sexy-as-god there wasn't much left of the fringe but scattered body parts. Striding forward, Brace had used his energy to hold the remaining Walker against the wall.

"What are you doing here?" he said to the passive man. "Were you working for Que? What was he trying to achieve?"

The man remained silent. He didn't shift or even blink. If I hadn't been able to see the rise and fall of his chest, I'd have thought he was dead.

I didn't move closer. Brace was giving off a leave-me-the-hell-alone vibe. As soon as I had this thought he shifted his head to shoot me a grin, and he was my warm heart-mate again. But really, he was scary when he went into Walker warrior mode.

Aribella.

The tapping on my mind shield and faint sound of my name alerted me to the fact that someone was trying to contact me. I lowered the shield.

Oh, thank the gods. I need your help. My mother's voice burst into my mind. She'd been trying hard to get through my barriers.

Where are you, Mom?

At the dark mountains. I'll meet you at the entrance.

I pulled my focus back to the room. "Luce, I have to leave; Mom needs my help on First World." I didn't give her any time to argue. "Colton, look after her and let Brace know where I'm going."

Call me if you need me, Red.

Brace must have heard me.

You got it.

I pictured the darkness surrounding the mountain and grabbed a large tether near the entrance. It was strange. Usually tethers were light and almost glittery, but here they seemed darker, and fragile. I worried I wouldn't make it, lost somewhere halfway if the tie broke. But I found myself arriving safely.

Lallielle was waiting as promised. She looked frazzled, her hair askew, shirt torn. In fact, I'd never seen my calm, collected mother look so out of sorts.

I dashed over to her side. Relief crossed her beautiful features when she saw me.

"What happened, Mom? Where's everyone else?"

She pulled me into a tight hug. "I've lost them. They just disappeared." Her voice was frantic over my shoulder. "I didn't know what to do or who else to ask."

I leaned out of the embrace. "I don't understand. Tell me what happened?"

"Let's head in now. We can talk while I take you to where I last saw them."

She hurried me into the darkened entrance. Last time Josian had lit the way, but since he wasn't there, my energy light ball was all we had.

"So we finished at Lucas' dance and came straight here. Quarn led the way with some of the royal guards. Apparently they had an idea where the corruption was coming from. We made it to that chamber with all the tunnels off it. You remember that we only explored two last time because Lucy said the rest were empty."

I nodded and she continued to speak. Her words were hurried, but still clear and articulate.

"Josian decided that we would quickly go down each of them, just to make sure there was nothing hidden. The first couple were dead ends. And then when we were halfway down the third I noticed that we were missing a few of our people. I didn't mention it in case I was wrong, but by the fourth there was no denying it."

"No one else noticed?" I asked.

She shrugged. "By the time I brought it up everyone was starting to question where people were."

She continued to push our pace and we soon crossed over that first doorway. I shuddered as I was hit with the negative energy again. There was so much on this side.

"Once we decided that people were disappearing, Quarn send a few of the guards back to find them, and they never returned. We were discussing what was happening when a noise had me spinning in the tunnel." She sniffed. "I had my back to the group for maybe a minute and when I turned around again, they were gone. Josian, Fury, Talli, Dune, and Quarn ... everyone ... they were all gone."

This wasn't the first time people had disappeared in these mountains. I worried at my lower lip, subconsciously picking up the pace.

I repeat, call me if you need help, Red.

I smiled, knowing that it went against Brace's control-freak personality to let me off on my own, but I liked that he trusted me.

I'm just helping with the tidy up here, he finished.

I shuddered at that mental image. There had been lots of body parts.

Well, so far there's something really off in these mountains but no immediate danger. I'll keep you updated.

He laughed. *How about I just stay in your head? You're notoriously bad at keeping in touch.*

He was right. I just got so caught up in the situation and forgot.

Lucy okay? I checked just before signing off.

Yep, no problems, unless you count the way she and Colt are snarling at each other.

So perfectly normal behavior by the sound of it.

I focused back on the mountain. Lallielle had my left hand squeezed tightly. She was probably afraid I'd disappear too. I was starting to get a bad feeling about what might have happened to all the people in these caves.

And the fact that Josian hadn't opened a doorway back was a little worrying.

But could they have disappeared into the wall here using the same trapdoor setup that I had fallen through on Regali? I knew that my journey through that door had something to do with the first Seventine, and this here felt like it might be something similar. It would certainly explain the vanishing-into-thin-air part.

We arrived in that large open space that had the dozen channels off it. Lallielle led me into the fifth one.

"This is where they disappeared," she whispered.

I tried to sense their energy, but there was nothing registering at all down there. We moved along the short length in no time. It was just a narrow, rock-lined tunnel. Nothing interesting, no spots of energy, just an empty tunnel.

It was on our second, slower trip along that I started to notice a strange pattern spanning the walls. Every four feet or so there was a slightly projected stone. I wouldn't have noticed if I hadn't been looking so closely, but it was definitely appearing at a regular interval.

And then suddenly in the center there was a space without one.

I ground to a halt.

Lallielle, who had not been expecting that, was jerked back by my hold on her hand. And it was at this point I felt the slightest of drafts from where we were standing.

"Do you feel that?" I said in a low voice near her ear.

She shifted on the spot, and didn't answer straight away. Then I felt her freeze.

"There's a breeze here." She let go of my hand and brought both of hers up to rest against the wall. "This has to be where they disappeared." She swung her head to face me. "In fact I think we were standing around this area."

I joined her in running my hands along the stone. This and the wall at Regali reminded me a lot of the entrances to the underground in Crais. I tried to remember what the inhabitants did there, how they had hidden the openings. Something to do with sliding one rock in front of the other.

Shifting my stance, I stopped trying to push against the wall and instead I tried to slide it. Straight away it shifted to the side. Lallielle almost fell through. I caught her at the last second.

"Damn," she swore. "How many of these secret entrances could be down here?"

"I have no idea." I poked my head around the corner.

It was another tunnel but I could see that there was light at the end. And as we stepped further in I could feel a cool breeze.

"There's something down that way. Let's go check it out."

I didn't have to worry about convincing her. Lallielle was moving faster than I was and she had her serious game face on. This was her protective mode. She was worried about our friends and family.

This tunnel was longer than number five, which ran adjacent to it. The light at the end was getting brighter and the air felt clear and cool. But it was a strange cool, almost like air-conditioning. But how could they have artificial air like that under a mountain?

And as we neared the end the smell hit me: chemicals. It smelt like the old medical wings in the orphanages. I had never quite figured out what caused that smell; probably something in the cleaning products.

Lallielle was still ahead of me. I heard her gasp and had to prevent myself from colliding with her as she stopped dead. I peered around her shoulder. My brain attempted to process the sensory information from my eyes, but it took me a few minutes to really register what I was seeing.

Brace. My tone was frantic. *I need you.*

Don't move. I'll be right there.

I reached out and stopped Lallielle before she stepped into the room. We both held our breath and waited.

The room of horror, as I had nicknamed it, was impossible to look at, and yet I couldn't take my eyes off the scene.

"Can you see Josian or the others?" Lallielle whispered.

She had tears trailing down her cheeks, just silent dripping tears that she did nothing to stem. I wanted to join her. I had that huge lump in my throat, burning eyes and gulping sensation that presaged tears, but really it was my pure rage that was keeping them at bay. How could anyone do this? Who was responsible for what we were seeing here? There was no indication at all of anyone in charge, no guards, nothing.

The sound of footsteps had us freezing.

I spun with my energy gathered.

I was pretty sure I knew who was coming but just in case. I relaxed as Brace ran into view. He dashed straight up to me, gathering me close. He must have had no problem with the trapdoor after I had explained it.

"Dammit, Red, your panic and pain is killing me." He ran one hand up and down my back. The other was around Lallielle's shoulders. "Calm yourself, baby," he whispered soothingly in my ear. "We'll figure out who's done this and they'll pay."

I could hear in his voice and feel through his shirt how rigid he was. His entire body was stonelike, but a stone that was vibrating at an impossible frequency. And I'd thought I was pissed off. Letting us go, he took one hesitant step into the white, sterile room. This impossible room that somehow existed in the middle of a mountain.

"It's safe; there's no warding; they didn't expect anyone to find this place." He waved us toward him. "And since Abernath's symbol coats the walls, I can only assume this was the work of Que, but who's been maintaining it since?"

Brace pointed out the intricate tribal mark that surrounded the entrance. I recognized the pattern from their banner at the gathering.

I gulped as I stepped closer. I didn't want the darkness there to touch me.

"What was he doing here? Why …?" I trailed off.

Brace shook his head as he stared around. "This is the large-scale version of what was happening on Earth in that warehouse. This is an energy slaughterhouse."

There were thousands of people. They hung in a type of suspended animation from the ceiling. Each had a slow steady drop of blood falling from a small incision in their neck. The blood landed on the floor, but then somehow was absorbed and white clean floors remained. The blood loss wouldn't be enough to kill them, but sufficient to keep them weak. I could see no other physical injuries, but small clouds of energy hovered visibly in front of their mouths. The dark, speckled hazes seemed to swell as the victims exhaled and then shrunk back again. And in the center of the ceiling, between all the bodies, a large shifting mass of energy resided.

"How long can they stay alive like this?" I choked out.

Lallielle just stood there, one hand covering her mouth, the other hanging listlessly at her side.

"First Worlders are the strongest of this star-system. I assume that's why he set it up here." Brace's words were harsh. "They regenerate and will last for a long time, but eventually, when the last tether is severed, they'll become the reanimated that we battled last time." He shook his head. "The Walkers here will never end; their energy just continues to renew itself. This is where he sent them," he muttered.

"What?" I said.

"Whenever someone disobeyed or failed Que, they disappeared. He said he was exiling them from Abernath, but they're here. I recognize many of them."

I choked back vomit again, that burning sensation rising in my throat. "So they've just been stuck hanging like this for hundreds of years."

Brace's eyes looked even blacker, if that was possible. "Yes, and the entire time they've been conscious and aware of what was happening to them."

"Where's Josian?" Lallielle suddenly sprang to life. "Where are Quarn and Fury, Talli and Dune? We have to find them."

"Wait here," Brace said and took off.

The bodies were suspended high enough that he could run under them and there was still a small gap. He used the path between them to avoid the small drops of blood. I could hear his footsteps through the cavernous hall and he was back by our sides in moments.

"They're not here, none of them," he said, his breathing even and calm. "But there looks to be another passage at the rear of this room. Let's see what's down there."

"What if the ones responsible are there?" I asked.

"I hope they are," he said darkly, leading us toward the far wall.

I tried not to look up as we walked, instead focusing on my feet, but for some reason my eyes were continually drawn toward the victims.

What a cruel way to be punished. And the First Worlders. I couldn't imagine … they just hung there until they were sucked dry of all their energy, and then when their last tether was severed they became reanimated. This place was a living tomb.

Finally we made it through. I let out the breath I hadn't even realized I'd been holding. The bright white light disappeared and we were back in a cave channel. This one was windy, and full of many bends. Still it didn't take long before we reached a barred door that sealed off the path. It was solid except for three bars that were too high for any of us – even Brace – to see in.

"There's a small energy field on it, but nowhere near strong enough to contain Josian if he was awake." Brace laid his hands on the stone. "Stand back."

"I can't feel him," Lallielle gasped out as we moved away from Brace. "And our bond is telling me nothing."

I could feel the electricity run down my arms at the buildup of Brace's power. I pulled Lallielle closer to me. With an echoing crack the door splintered down the center; Brace used both hands to wedge a gap large enough for us to enter.

"I'll go first. Wait for me to check it out," he said as he entered the room.

Completely ignoring him, Lallielle and I pushed our way in behind him. With a sigh he held out a hand and helped us through. He leaned down to kiss my cheek.

"Never change, Red," was all he said before turning away to observe the room.

It was dimly lit. I couldn't see much, but as we stepped further in Brace shot out a blast of bright light that illuminated the entire area. A crouched person turned to face us. She was surrounded by bodies. And as my eyes adjusted I realized what I was seeing. Josian's fiery blood-red hair was a splash of color in an otherwise gray room. Beside him were Quarn, Talina, Fury and Dune. I locked eyes with the woman who had been shifting the bodies.

"You've got to be effing kidding me," I said.

Chapter 9

She stood and faced us. Her arrogant features were expressionless and she held a blade in her right hand. Her movements were strong and calm as she stepped free of the bodies. My blood boiled. She showed not one iota of distress that she was currently standing over our unmoving loved ones.

"Well, look who it is," she finally drawled, her slicked-back black hair framing her bony features. "Abigail the orphan."

Patricia Olden, a woman who I'd thought we were long ago rid of, the very one who had plunged a knife into my chest, was looking whole and healthy.

I thought it was going to be Brace who moved first, but it was Lallielle. Just like on Earth, she had her fist back, swinging a punch at Olden. But somehow the evil harpy dodged my mother and with quick movements shoved her aside. Lallielle flew into the pile of bodies. I narrowed my eyes. That had been unnaturally fast and strong.

"She's all hopped up on energy, right?" I asked.

Brace gave me a quick look out of the corner of his eye, the edge of his mouth just lifting slightly.

"Yes," Olden answered. "There's so much free energy, and they don't mind me borrowing some."

Lallielle was moving around on the floor, her hands fluttering over Josian. She smiled at me, so I hoped that meant he was okay.

"Who is 'they', Olden?" I turned back to her. "Who's pulling your strings? I thought it was Que."

She laughed. "Still stupid, I see."

I'd have been offended except I didn't give a shit what she thought of me.

"Que was just a lackey like me." She paused. "Well, maybe with a bit more power, but at the end of the day we all work for someone else."

"Who?" Brace stepped closer, his fists clenched.

Olden glared at him. "Well, if it isn't Que's son. He was so proud when you snapped my neck." She rubbed at her throat. "We never did get along. Lucky I was more useful to the head honchos alive than dead; bit of energy and here I am to tell this story."

"She's stalling us," I muttered to Brace.

"I know." He dived across the room and, unlike Lallielle's attack, his didn't miss. He scooped Olden up, one hand around her throat as he slammed her against the wall. Her knife fell uselessly to the floor.

"Here we are again." He grinned up at her. "And this time I'll break you into so many pieces you won't be coming back."

While Brace had her occupied I sprinted to Lallielle.

"Are they okay?" I asked.

"Yes," she said, "I think it's some type of drug keeping them unconscious."

What?

"How could any drug work on a Walker?" I checked Talina. Her breathing seemed light but regular. "I didn't think that was possible."

"E … En … Energy."

I turned to face Olden as she spluttered. Brace loosened his grip.

"If you mix energy with regular old Earth kepta it knocks a Walker out for hours. Gives me enough time to prepare them for the room."

I gasped. Kepta was the drug of choice amongst the gangers of Earth. It was a mist contained in small canisters. If used within a one-hour period, one spray gave a euphoric high, two sprays knocked you unconscious and three was death. A most dangerous but useful drug. And it was easy to store and carry.

"That's why you were brought in," I said as dots started to connect in my head. "They needed your gang connections to find the kepta."

She laughed. "Wrong again. My father created kepta and I'm the one who holds the knowledge of its formula. Gangers are filthy, stupid creatures. I have no use for them."

She was being awfully chatty. Why was she telling us all this? It almost felt as if she'd been … lonely. She wanted to tell someone what she'd been up to.

"Have you been stuck under here since we found the warehouse on Earth?"

She locked me into her dark evil eyes. "Yes. Once the warehouse was discovered they wanted to shift everything here. Keep it under wraps."

"What was the point of the Earth one, anyways?" Brace asked.

"They needed me to keep an eye on Abigail until she reached her enlightenment." Olden tried to swallow around Brace's hand. The action looked painful. "And then the next part of their plan could work or something."

"I'm sure she only knows basic information," Lallielle said. "No one would tell a lackey anything important."

"Arghhh."

I jumped as Josian roared to life – literally. And he was not happy. Lallielle dived out of the way as he started thrashing around.

"Josian ... Jos!" she shouted. "You're okay."

The moment he heard her voice he calmed. The flashing bronze of his eyes dulled as a semblance of humanity bled back into them.

"Where am I? What happened?" He was already on his feet as he asked. "Why is she still alive?" He pulled Lallielle into his arms, his calm growing even further.

Despite his disorientation when he awoke, you could tell he'd still assessed the scene and drawn conclusions.

"Don't worry; she won't be for much longer," Brace said calmly.

"I can tell you things," Olden said, sounding worried for the first time. "Do you want to know what they're doing with all this energy? What happens to those subjects after they've been drained?"

"The energy is for releasing the Seventine and the drained turn into reanimated," Brace answered.

Her eyes registered surprise.

"See, I don't think you can tell us anything important. If I know my father, he didn't tell you shit, and if he isn't even the top dog then Lalli is right: you won't know anything."

"How much damn energy is needed to release them?" I asked, thinking of the mass back in the other room. And who knew how long this had been going on.

"A lot, baby girl," Josian said, "the original seven wanted it to be very difficult to release the Seventine; practically impossible. I'm starting to think that the Walkers were right, the level of energy required to lock them away is what caused the originals' disappearance."

"If you free me I'll show you Samuel," Olden piped up. "And without me you'll never save him."

Everyone froze.

Lallielle was the only one whose expression changed. I'm not sure what the others were thinking but that didn't sound like a bargaining chip to me.

"If you find Sammy and help me save him, I will not kill you." Brace shocked the hell out of me with those words.

"Brace," I bit out, "he was the one who facilitated your possession by the Seventine. We owe him nothing."

Brace's expression softened. "I understand, Abbs. If someone had taken you from me, I don't think I'd be so forgiving, but Sammy was my friend for a long time and I know how easy it can be to be manipulated by powerful people. He deserves a chance to explain himself, don't you think?"

Damn Brace, making me think and feel things I didn't want to.

"Fine, be the mature grown-up one." I sniffed. "Just remember a few hours ago you were a tornado ripping pack people to bits."

Brace grinned at me, and lowered Olden to the ground. Her hands rose to rub at her neck.

"As long as Abby doesn't get hurt, then the angry Brace stays controlled." He got in close to Olden's bony face. "Keep that in mind."

"If you needed to keep me alive on Earth then why did you stab me?" I was trying to figure out her motivation.

She laughed; it was raspy; Brace had hurt her throat. "I knew that wouldn't kill you. It was just fun to inflict pain."

At that moment I may have lost it a little and I may have punched her in the nose.

Brace laughed as he lifted me off her with one hand. With the other he grabbed her arm roughly. "Start moving or I'll let Red loose on you again."

We moved back toward the white room, Lallielle looking both nervous and hopeful. This was the closest she'd come to getting her son back.

"I'll stay here," Josian said. "I'll join you after I wake them." He waved toward the others, who were still unconscious.

We nodded. Lallielle dashed back for one last kiss.

"I love you," I heard Josian murmur to her as he gently caressed her face.

Lallielle was much more herself as we left that barred room and marched back to the room of horror. Brace still had a firm grip around Olden. I doubted she could outrun anyone here, but he was taking no chances. She'd been partaking of energy for a long time, and I had no idea what the side-effects of that would be.

Nothing was said as Olden pointed toward the far left corner; we just kept moving across. The vacant expressions of the victims haunted me as we continued to pass under them. And then, after many nameless strangers, I finally saw them; Samuel and Francesca were suspended side by side.

"Frannie as well." Lalllielle gasped. "But when I asked about her, Lucy said she was happy."

I think what Lucy had actually said was that Frannie was not unhappy, but still I understood Lallielle's point. This was far from either.

"She doesn't know what's happening. They're living in dream worlds," Olden said. "The hovering energy keeps all First Worlders from awareness, which is much better than the Walkers' experience." She smirked at me. "We can keep them immobile, but they're fully sentient during the entire procedure. We've found nothing to cloud their minds."

That was interesting since I knew my dream power could do just that.

"I hope you know that you are going to hell." I bared my teeth at her.

"You can't hurt me. You promised." Her eyes widened.

It was a nice change having some of the power. As a child, I'd spent too many years letting this woman push me around.

I laughed. It echoed around the cavernous hall. "No, I didn't."

"Well, you still need me to help save these two. The severing of tethers is generally irreversible. All of these First Worlders will die."

"The girls from the compound didn't die on Earth," I said, my brow furrowed.

"It wasn't the same process. Earthlings are weak. I was simply draining their energy. That was the only way to get anything from them."

"How do we save them?" Lallielle asked, her tearful face looking up at her son and sister. "I need you to tell me now."

Olden did not hesitate, opening her mouth immediately. Why was she so free with this information? It was making me nervous.

"You need to sacrifice someone," she said.

And there was my answer.

"The tethers which have been severed from these two must be replaced with tethers from another First Worlder, and they must volunteer for the sacrifice. There's no other way to save them." She sounded so pleased with herself.

I don't hate many people, but I truly hated her. She'd given Lallielle hope, and then in one moment dashed it away.

"And while you're mulling that over, I've decided to add a little more distress and tell you what powerful entity is the brains behind the release of the Seventine. Why? Well, because there's nothing you can do to stop them. Their power is beyond anything you could imagine and you don't stand a chance."

She smiled. "I love that you will feel helpless, and the best part is you haven't even questioned why now, of all times in the past and future, they have chosen this moment to –"

She was opening her mouth to continue speaking when her eyes rolled back in her head. She gasped once or twice, her face turning an interesting shade of burnt umber, and then she started to scream.

We all jumped back as she began to disintegrate in on herself. Like she was melting.

"What's happening?" Josian asked as he ran up.

Behind him were the rest of our friends. Talina, Quarn, Fury and Dune. They looked a little dazed, but I couldn't see any other damage.

"I don't know." Lallielle started to fret. "She was just speaking and then … she's disappearing."

"She was destroyed," I said, staring down at the puddle of goo she was becoming, "because she was telling us too much."

"Yes, she was about to reveal who was behind it all," Brace said, clenching his fists, his frustration spilling over.

Lallielle shook her head. "I don't believe that she truly knew any more than that Que wasn't the biggest power. What I want to know is how do we save Sammy and Frannie?"

"We need to figure out how to save them all," Fury spit out, waving toward the thousands of suspended bodies.

She was so angry, her hands were claws and her dark eyes narrowed. I guessed she also hadn't appreciated being knocked out.

"This is the worst thing I've ever seen, and we were about to become one of these husks." She threw her hands in the air, her body encased in her blue flames.

"Fury, calm, baby. Otherwise you are going to hurt someone." Dune, who could touch her without burning himself, was running both hands up and down her arms.

She breathed in deeply, although it didn't seem to be making it any better. I understood her feelings: it was hard to calm down when faced with this room.

"What did she say about saving them?" Josian turned to Lallielle, his generally jovial features creased with concern.

"She said that we needed to find a First Worlder to volunteer to sacrifice themselves so that their tethers could replace the ones lost from … my family." Lallielle reached out a hand toward the suspended victims, but she couldn't quite reach Samuel's foot.

The look on her face was pure devastation. I hoped I never had to lose a child. I knew I wouldn't survive it and Lallielle had done it twice in her lifetime.

We were all quiet. I was considering the impossibilities of saving them. I knew Lallielle would never sacrifice another, and who would volunteer for something so –?

"I'll do it."

My breath caught in my throat at the sound of his words. Tears already filled my eyes as I faced him, and I was subconsciously shaking my head from side to side.

My guardian caught my eye; his piercing blue were flooded with sadness.

"No," I whispered. "I need you."

He moved forward and took my hands into his weathered ones. "I have watched over you for years. After losing my Hallow that was the only thing that kept me moving forward. I'm tired, Aribella, you are safe with your family and you have grown up so beautiful and strong. You don't need me anymore."

He shifted his head slightly to face the wide, stricken eyes of his oldest friend. "And if I can make this sacrifice for my loved ones I can think of no better way to join my Hallow."

"I will not," Lalllielle said strongly. "I couldn't live with myself." She turned away. "And I'm not even sure either of them deserve a sacrifice."

"It is not your decision to make," he said firmly. "And despite my personal feelings for the woman,

I do think Francesca is very important; she foresaw this entire thing."

He turned his back on Lallielle. "Do you know how to reverse their tethers and replace them with mine?" he asked Josian.

Josian regarded the devastation on his mate's features for a brief moment before facing Quarn. "I don't think this is the right decision. You have many who love you, but it's not my place to intercede in this choice if you've made it. I've seen something like this once, performed by one of the ancient ones. If you're serious about this I'll go find him."

Quarn nodded his head firmly. "Yes, get him."

Lallielle stepped forward. "I'm begging you not to assist him in this foolish plan."

I lent my support to her words by taking her hand.

She continued. "He's always been a self-sacrificing person. It's part of his gift as a protector and what made him such a perfect guardian. But he doesn't always make rational decisions."

"Still standing right here, Lalli," Quarn said with a grin. "And you know my sacrifice could save more than just two. Depending on their tether loss, I could save many."

Brace cleared his throat. "Don't diminish his gift. Take joy in the choice he's making; it's a most honorable way to die."

I glared at him. "What?" I mean seriously. "I hope you're kidding, Brace, otherwise you and I are going to have a serious problem."

Brace and Josian genuinely looked confused. They couldn't understand why Lallielle and I were so upset.

"Is it not honorable to die and save many?" Brace asked. "Walkers will release their energy if the cause is important enough."

"It's honorable to live for those that you love," Lallielle choked out.

Quarn's eyes looked crestfallen. "Would you really punish me to a thousand lifetimes without Hallow? I am ready to release my essence and have new life reborn, or in my case restore life to those who had it brutally stolen."

He'd struck a chord with Lallielle now. I could see the resignation on her features, followed by the hot, heavy tears that signified her moment of acceptance. She was a First Worlder. They had a great understanding of life and how endless time wasn't always a gift.

But I had been raised on Earth. We fought and scraped to stay alive. We lived every moment. And I was not okay with this.

181

Without another word I wrenched myself free from my mother and turned to leave the room of horrors. They could make whatever decision they wanted, but I wasn't standing around and watching my guardian die.

As soon as I was out of the room I traced back to Regali.

Abby.

Brace's voice was soft.

Get out of my head, and don't follow me. I want to be alone. I all but screamed the words at him before slamming down my shields.

I knew it wasn't his fault. I was just so hurt and angry, and when I'd needed his support he'd sided with Quarn.

I was in Ria's home, just standing there staring into nothing. I had traced there in the faint hope that I would find Lucy; she would understand.

"Abbs?"

I spun around and threw myself at Lucy.

"What happened? Is everyone okay?" Her voice sounded frantic over my shoulder. "You haven't been gone long."

It felt as if I'd been gone a thousand years.

Colton sidled out of the darkened room behind us. Ria followed him. I lifted my head to give them both a tear-stained smile.

"Sorry, I just busted in here without warning."

Lucy was now holding me at arm's length. "Tell me what happened," she said as she shook me.

Pulling away, I started to pace the hard wood floor. I quickly detailed everything that had happened since I had left.

Ria remained quiet. This problem didn't mean anything to her. Lucy had both hands on her face, and her mouth open, and Colton leaned somberly against the wall. Finally I finished by choking out Quarn's stupid plan. I brushed away the angry tears that wet my eyes.

"Are. You. Freaking. Kidding. Me?" Lucy's blue eyes were wide and shiny. "Oh, Ralph won't have to kill himself; I'll do it for him being such a dumbass."

"I don't understand the problem –" Colton started.

I waved my hand to cut him off.

"Ignore the Walker men. They're high on opinions and short on brains."

Lucy forced a chuckle. "Brace is in trouble."

I growled. "I don't want to talk about it."

"Can we stop Quarn?" Lucy asked.

I gulped down a few times. "I don't think so. He looked serious, and he misses Hallow. I think he truly believes that this is what his destiny is now."

"It is honorable," Colton managed to spit out between our glares.

I rested my head on my hands. "If I have to hear that stupid word one more time."

"I think, Abbs," Lucy said as she reached out and took my hands from my face, "that maybe you should go back. You don't want to miss saying goodbye to Quarn."

"My heart hurts," I whimpered. "I don't want to feel this. Why can't everyone just stay alive and be happy?"

She sighed. "I don't want to be a bitch on top of everything, but you're thinking like a child. We're fighting a huge battle. There are going to be deaths, sacrifices. It's inevitable."

I stomped my foot hard. "I don't accept that, and even if I did this isn't a random, violent, unavoidable death. This is Quarn making the actual choice. He's choosing this."

"Yes, but if he didn't choose this, Frannie and Sammy would both die," Lucy said.

And I realized that she'd been pretty cagey about how she felt about Samuel's involvement.

I guess what it really boiled down to was the fact that I loved Quarn, and I didn't love either Frannie or Samuel. To me, my loved one was worth more than any other, but Lucy was right: I was thinking like a child.

"I have to go back," I whispered.

"We'll go with you," Lucy said.

Colton just nodded, reaching out to take my free hand.

"I will wait here for your return. We have much to discuss regarding the Seventine and the fringe," Ria said.

She'd been so quiet during my meltdown I'd almost forgotten she was there.

"We'll see you soon." I smiled at her.

Clutching my friends close, I pictured the room of horrors. I hesitated briefly before reaching toward a tether close to the door. It was time to trace us back.

Chapter 10

I didn't want to walk into the room. Colton and Lucy were hovering at the edge of the doorway, their faces reflecting the horror I could never forget. I knew they wouldn't be able to see our family back in their far corner, so there was no point asking if Quarn was dead yet.

I felt Brace's energy then. He was moving toward me.

"You should go back there, Abby, he's waiting for you." His deep tones washed away some of my ragged edges.

I felt relief and dread; I wasn't too late. I had my head against the rock wall, my eyes closed so I couldn't see Brace.

"I know it hurts," he continued. "And I'm sure it's the last thing you want to do, but if you don't say goodbye you'll always regret it."

He didn't touch me, which I both needed and would also hate right now, but he was sending warm waves of loving energy toward me. I pushed myself off the wall and my eyes caught on his face. The hurt I saw there, in the dark depths of his eyes, almost had me caving, but my righteous anger dulled it enough that I could stride past without reaching out to touch him.

Lucy and Colton followed as I marched toward the small group still huddled in the far corner. Josian's red hair was the first thing to come into view. I could see he was talking to a Walker, a man who wore the indigo marks of Whar. I realized it was Ria's father, Nos.

"Aribella!" Josian exclaimed as I moved into view. "Come say hello to Nos." He waved me toward them.

Lucy and Colton left me to join the others and I stepped up to the two imposing Walkers. Josian showed no negative emotion regarding my earlier departure. I never felt judged by Josian, just love and acceptance. Rare even from one's father.

I hadn't paid much attention to Nos at the gathering, but now I could see that he looked like the male version of Ria: the same stunning features and tawny-colored skin. And those purple eyes were watching me without even a single blink to break their stare.

"Hello, nice to see you again," I said, my voice hoarse and flat.

"How did you find Regali and my daughter?" His voice was deep.

I threw a confused look toward Josian. How the hell had he –?

"Nos is a visionary. It's the Walker version of a soothsayer. He's the one I've called for help in transferring the tethers."

I examined him closer. "Have you had a vision of this happening?" I questioned.

He shook his head. "No, it doesn't work like that for me. I have a vision about once every hundred years, but sometimes I just know things." He paused. "I'm more of a history record keeper. There's only one living Walker visionary. The successor is appointed upon the death of the predecessor. And you know you're the visionary because at that moment all the knowledge of all previous visionaries is passed to you."

"That's how you knew so much at the gathering." And still he had not thought to tell me that his daughter was the half-Walker I would seek on Regali. Damn Walkers and their secrecy.

He nodded. "Yes, I hold the memory and history of hundreds of lives. It can get very hard to remember which memories are my own and which I inherited."

"How long have you been the visionary?"

He blinked a few times. "I don't know exactly." He finally muttered, "A long time."

"And now you're here to kill Quarn?" I said bluntly.

"Aribella." Quarn walked over from where he'd been hovering close by. "No one has to kill me. It is a simple process – like going to sleep."

"Yeah, going to sleep and never waking up," I mumbled.

"I do have this knowledge you seek, although I've never performed a tether transfer," Nos admitted.

"How many people will you save?" I had to know it was worth it, that my harsh, bossy, crazily protective guardian's death was worth it.

"On top of Samuel and Francesca, there'll be enough tethers to save ten others with similar losses to your brother and aunt," Nos said.

I didn't bother to correct him on the brother and aunt thing; those two were not my family.

It was now or never. There was no more time with Quarn. I took a deep breath and launched myself at him.

"Please. Please," I begged. "Please don't do this. I need you." Tears and desperation poured out of me.

I knew it was fruitless, but I had to try. The others were right, though. Despite the fact I hated the word, Quarn was an honorable man and he would never walk away from this sacrifice.

"Aribella, I wish I could stay and help you save the world. But if there is one thing I have learnt from my years with you, it's that you don't need me. You mostly saved yourself. I just got to witness all of the wonder."

He pulled me tighter into the hug. "I never had a child. Hallow didn't want to take free energy from others, but you have been a daughter to me and I will always be with you. My tethers go to these people but my free energy will be reborn. I will find my Hallow again and the cycle will continue. This is the great life plan."

I couldn't speak, I was crying so hard. Eventually Josian had to take me away. He gathered me in his big body and gave one of those bear hugs that he's so good at.

"I can't stand by and watch her pain any longer." I could hear Brace's terse tone. It sounded as if someone was holding him back.

"Right now she's angry and upset. Give her space." Colton's voice was low.

"No."

He was stubborn. And he was mine, for now at least. Unless the ritual worked, I'd soon be losing

Brace also. My mind shied away from that. I wasn't strong enough to handle it.

"It's time." Nos interrupted my morbid thoughts. "I must return to my clan. We were in the middle of an important meet when Josian collected me."

Damn, Walkers were also rude.

"That's a true Walker," I heard Lucy say. "Wham, bam, thank you, mam."

I don't think most of them got the reference.

"I am an important person," Nos stated.

And there was no snooty tone, just spoken as if it were a fact. No one bothered to argue. The arrogance of Walkers was solid, and arguing just gave me a headache.

"What will happen to the rest of those in here?" I indicated the thousands of bodies.

There was a pause. No one wanted to answer, and I had a sick feeling what that meant.

"The Walkers are being awoken. They have no tethers and will make a full recovery once their energy is allowed to replenish," Josian said.

"And the rest ... the First Worlders," I prompted.

Lallielle walked up then. Her face was almost haggard in the harsh white light. She might have accepted Quarn's decision, but she wasn't happy about it.

"They'll be destroyed." Her voice wavered. She cleared her throat. "If we wake them they'll die slowly without all their tethers and turn into the reanimated dead."

"Well, that's a bitch." I shook my head.

There was really nothing more to say.

Nos led us over to the spot under Samuel and Francesca. My understanding was that Quarn's tethers would spread to them first and then branch out to find those closest that needed them.

"Okay, it's time to say goodbye." Nos gave one nod.

I stared at the floor while Quarn made the rounds. Brace was right behind me. I could feel him, but he was still respecting my need to be mad at him right then and didn't touch me. Lucy clung to Quarn for a long moment, her pale features red and swollen with tears.

"You stay strong, Miss Lucy," I heard Quarn say. "You and Aribella have a special relationship and it is this strength which will make the difference in the end."

"I love you, Ralph," she said when she eventually pulled back.

Finally it was my turn.

I didn't lift my eyes at first. I focused on his worn boots instead.

"Where is my brave Abigail?" he said.

My eyes flew up. He didn't usually call me by my Earth name.

"There, that's better." His blue eyes drilled into me. "I have one last piece of advice for you. People will come in and out of your life, make you promises that you know in your heart are false. Trust in yourself, trust in your heart and you will never be wrong." He leaned in close to me. "Beware the tides of Lucas."

I pulled back to see his face better. "What does that mean?"

"There is something there. I don't know what it is, but I just don't want you to let your guard down with him."

I nodded. That was something easy to promise.

"Well, my dear girl, this is farewell for now. I will see you again in another life." He leaned down and kissed my cheeks and then my forehead.

I closed my eyes as he lingered there for a moment, breathing in the scent of Quarn. He was the first person to give me hope, the one to bring me to my life.

"I'll see you again," I promised him. "You and I are a team, Quarn."

"Yes, we are."

I turned away then, allowing him to move to Lallielle.

"Don't say anything." She held up her hand. "This is my fault. I should never have sent you and Hallow to Earth. I made the wrong decision. I deserve to lose you too."

He laughed. It sounded loud and grating in the cavernous hall. "Maybe you do need me to stick around and knock some sense into you. I have never blamed you. Fate is not yours to circumvent, and your actions probably saved more lives than you know."

"Always and forever," Lallielle said as they touched foreheads.

"Always and forever," he repeated back to her, and for the first time a tear trailed down his cheek.

Brace's arms encircled me. I sank into his comfort.

"I'm sorry, baby, I'm so sorry." He sounded sad.

I just pulled his arms tighter around me.

Nos had stepped up to Quarn now. I had to fight the urge to dash forward and rip them apart. Quarn locked eyes with me and I knew this was the last moment I would see that piercing blue. Lallielle was sobbing into Josian's shirt front. She didn't seem to want to look, but I couldn't take my eyes off them.

Quarn gave me one last nod before turning away and facing forward. Nos leaned in close and with a few low words, which I couldn't hear, energy encased Quarn. His eyes closed and I heard the breath expel from his body. I waited for it to sound again, but it didn't.

I bit back a moan of pain, watching as Quarn's body started to rise. Suddenly there were visible tethers coming off him, at least twenty different ones. The cords stretched out and as he rose three attached to Samuel, two to Francesca and the rest to seven of the people around him. At the same time, the thousands of other bodies around us started lowering to the ground.

Fully visible on the now empty ceiling, the mass of energy which was gathered in the center of the room shifted, and for some reason I had pull myself from Brace's arms and move toward it. I don't know what made me do it, but I threw out my golden cord and without pause it extended itself and attached to the pulse of energy.

I hit the ground, landing on my knees.

I'd never felt a bulk of power like this. It was a living entity. It could create and destroy and level this world to the ground.

The well inside me jumped to attention. It was happy right now and it wanted the energy. I started to draw it into me, waves and flows, masses of power. I didn't know who I was anymore. There was nothing separating me and the energy. It took forever or seconds. I had no indication of time passing, but finally I swallowed the last bit of mist.

"Get rid of it, Red. Release that power or it will kill you." Brace's words finally broke through the silent bubble that had been encasing me.

And now I could feel the mass pulsing inside me. It was going to kill me; I could feel the laboring of my heart.

I had no choice.

"Protect Lucy," I screamed.

I couldn't hold it any longer, and released it in one large explosion.

Even though it had been floating on the ceiling before I'd tethered to it, it must have still been contained somehow. But now I'd set it free and it streamed out to connect with every person in the room.

The unconscious Walkers sprang to life, and they weren't the only ones. The First Worlders opened their eyes. I watched in astonishment as every victim awoke, and not as reanimated beings, but as themselves.

I had my hands resting on my knees as I leaned forward and huffed in some deep breaths. Without even realizing it, or knowing what I'd done, life had been restored.

I swung my head around to where Quarn's body had come to rest. But, unlike everyone else, he was still on the ground, his corpse colorless.

I ran to him.

"Quarn," I yelled as I skidded on my knees next to his body. I grabbed his hand, squeezing it tightly. "Wake up, please."

I wasn't above begging. He didn't have to die that day.

"Why didn't anyone tell me I could do that?" I screamed. "Why wasn't that the first option?"

"Because that's never been done before." Nos was the one who answered. "No one in our history, even the originals, could have taken a mass of free energy and actually returned it to the rightful owners. Tethers cannot be restored like that, only by way of sacrifice."

As usual I'd learnt something just moments too late. But as I had that thought Quarn coughed. I gasped as color flooded back into his features. I threw myself down on him.

"Thank you, thank you," I kept whispering.

The room around us exploded with noise and confusion.

Everyone else, except for Brace, Colton and Lucy, moved forward to deal with the crazy bedlam of this awakening. The three stood behind me and Quarn like bodyguards. They didn't leave our sides. Lallielle came to sit across from me and took his hand into hers.

"A hundred and forty-seven years of friendship." Her voice was stern as she held his hand. "You're lucky that Aribella figured out how to save everyone."

"What happened?" His piercing blue eyes held confusion. "I don't seem to be dead."

I laughed. "Sorry, buddy, not on my watch."

He pulled himself up to a sitting position. His eyes darting around as he took in the crying, screaming and thoroughly confusing chaos around us.

"Well, I am glad my sacrifice wasn't in vain," he muttered. "How are Samuel and Francesca?" Lallielle shrugged. "I haven't had a chance to see them. I was more worried that my oldest friend was dead."

"Abbs." Lucy interrupted us. "While it's great that you didn't bite the dust, Ralph, we really have to go back to Regali and convince Ria to leave."

She was right; I was running out of time for the fourth ritual.

"Promise me you won't do anything stupid while I'm gone." I glared at my guardian as we both stood.

He laughed. "Can't promise that, but I can promise I'll be here when you return."

Everyone gathered around me. I got a big hug from an unusually pale Talina. She kind of laughed and cried as she pulled me closer.

"Thank you ... thank you ... thank you." Her words were low and mumbled so it took me a few moments to figure out what she was saying.

I pulled back so I could see her face. "What are you thanking me for?"

And just as I asked I saw him.

The mass of blue hair hung in lank strands down his back, but there was no mistaking the lashless yellow eyes of the Spurn native. Ladre.

"He was here, his energy being drained, and you gave him back his life," Talina practically gushed.

"But how?" I said, shaking my head. "He should have dried out months ago."

"The sleep stasis they were all in was like a vacuum. They didn't age or grow or change. Although I'm not sure how much longer he could have lasted without water," Brace answered.

Talina leaned in close to me again.

"Can you take us to the ocean, Abbs?"

I held out my hand to her and we sprinted to Ladre. He grabbed Talina's free hand without hesitation.

"Hold on," I said, before tracing them straight to our ocean house in Angelisian.

Ladre didn't even pause. The instant he saw the water he took off. Talina stayed back for an extra few moments.

"Will you be okay?" Her warm brown eyes were sad. "I want to go with you, but Ladre needs me right now."

I shooed her away. "I'll be back soon, hopefully with Ria so we can perform the fourth ritual. For now, you go and enjoy your reunion."

I was so happy for her. I'd really thought Ladre was dead so this was amazing.

She dashed into the water where her mer-man was waiting for her. No doubt they'd be gone for a while. Talina had assured me many times that there were similar krill animals in this ocean to those on Spurn, so they wouldn't starve.

I traced back to the room of horror. They were still waiting for me. I could see Lallielle speaking to her sister. Francesca looked a little shell-shocked, her white hair straggly around her face. Samuel sat on the floor near them, but at this stage no one was close to him. I strode right up to him. As he saw me coming he got to his feet.

"Aribella, wait. I need to explain." He held both hands up in front of him, but I didn't care.

I punched him straight in the nose. I put every ounce of my anger and hurt into the swing and was satisfied to hear a distinct crunching sound.

"Explain away," I said as I turned my back on him and walked away.

Josian grinned at me. Lallielle looked upset but resigned. She had been expecting that by the looks.

Lucy gave me a high five when I reached her side. "You beat me to it, plastic surgeon."

Yep, I could add another broken nose to my tally. It was at that moment, I think, whilst holding his freely bleeding face, that Samuel realized Lucy was in the room with him.

I heard her soft gasp as he locked eyes with her. And there was something there. His eyes blazed with emotion and suddenly it looked like our theories were wrong. I don't think Samuel had been using her at all. If that look was any indication ... he loved her.

And suddenly Colton was at her side.

Oh no, the shit was going to hit the ceiling now.

Lucy wasn't speaking. It was one of those rare occasions when she was speechless, although her cheeks were flushed.

"So we have to go back to Regali. Who's coming this time?" I broke the weird standoff.

The low rumbles coming from Colton were getting quite distinctive.

"I'll be there, of course." Brace gave me a half-grin.

"Count me in," Colton growled.

"I'm in, of course," Lucy agreed.

"I think we might stay here again," Fury said. "I'm still feeling the after-effects of the drug. I'm not really up to it."

Dune nodded.

Samuel was still watching us, but thankfully for his personal health he never approached.

"Keep an eye on Samuel for me," I asked Fury.

She knew the story so she understood my worries.

"I'm sure he'll have a convincing excuse for Mom, and I don't want everyone to let their guard down," I finished.

"You got it," she promised.

I gave Lallielle and Josian quick hugs, explaining I was leaving for Regali.

"Be careful," Josian said, "we'll be here cleaning this up for a while, but I can come at any time that you need me."

Ignoring the watchful and freaky white eyes of Francesca, I grabbed Brace, Lucy and Colton, preparing to trace them to Regali. I knew I'd hear the soothsayer's story when I got back, but right then I had more important things to deal with.

Chapter 11

Ria hadn't seemed to mind the last time, so I just traced us straight into her home. I was hoping that we could save some time, but the tree-house seemed to be empty. I glanced out of the open window. The vines were spread out instead of falling to shield the forest. I'd grown used to the odd blue tint of the world in Regali, but strangely enough it seemed as if it the light filtering through the canopy was now purple.

That was odd.

Colton and Lucy seemed to be in the middle of a terse conversation. Brace gave me a grin over the top of their heads before crossing around them to stand at the window with me. We stood there for a few minutes in silence. But just because we were silent didn't mean everything was. The jungle seemed extra noisy with animal calls and rustling.

"Are we okay, Red?" Brace finally spoke.

Turning from the view, I faced him. The purple lighting highlighted the dark beauty that was all Brace. Need slammed into me with a speed that literally took my breath away. I'd been so steadfastly ignoring our bond when I was angry, but now, as it roared back to life, I couldn't stop myself from diving into his arms. And as they closed around me I could finally breathe again.

"I need to know that you don't doubt us. I might not always have the same opinion as you, but I'll always have your back," he said. "You can't shut me out like that anymore, though."

"I was really not okay with Quarn's decision," I said. "And I'm not sure I accept or understand how you could agree with him, but I have to respect everyone's right to make choices and have a differing opinion."

"It's not so much that I agreed with him, more along the lines that I understood his reasoning. And I believe every man has the right to make choices such as those."

"Every *man* has the right? What about women?"

He paused, I'm sure to weigh up which words wouldn't get him into more trouble.

"Women are rare, precious and absolutely essential to the survival of all creatures. They can't

204

die unnecessarily." He moved closer to my ear, his breath fanning over me.

I shivered in response.

"I just don't want anyone I love to die." I sounded like a whiny five-year-old who wanted the happily-ever-after in the fairytale.

"I'll do my best to keep everyone kicking –" Brace was cut off by angry voices.

"I told you it's none of your business."

Lucy was in full virago mode. I could see where she'd mussed her blond curls everywhere in her frustration.

I don't know what Colton had been saying previously, but when he spoke again his voice was dead calm.

"You're right, Lucy, just be careful. I don't like the way he was looking at you." He left her side and stood next to Brace.

There was no expression on his gorgeous, icy features.

Lucy looked a little shocked, eventually making her way to our side also. She threw a few confused glances in his direction, but no more was said on the matter of Samuel.

"Don't let that asshat ruin your friendship with Colt," I said in a low voice to Lucy.

She sighed. "He has no right to question my life. He didn't want to be a part of it. He's broken, or whatever crap he talks about, so he can keep his opinions to himself."

"Standing right here and can hear exceptionally well," Colton said, staring forward. Although the slightest grin might have crossed his lips.

"Should we go down into the jungle and look for Ria?" I peered out into the noisy rainforest.

"That would be a bad idea."

The words sounded from behind us. We all spun around to find Ria jumping into the room from a side branch.

"It is the red moon tonight. The packs have shifted into their animal forms and are running through Artwon." She stood before us, naked as the day she was born, and damn, the woman could rock some curves.

I fought the instinct to reach up and cover Brace's eyes, but in the end I was okay with it. I wasn't an insecure person and I knew he loved me. Melded mates didn't have much room in a relationship for jealousy, our bond was too great. Lucy clearly didn't feel the same way. She wiggled around and elbowed Colton in the ribs.

"Sorry about that, didn't see you there," she said.

"Of course not." I laughed. "Six and half feet and two hundred pounds of man always blends into the scenery."

"I'm sorry." Ria laughed. It was a light sound that echoed around her space. "I didn't stop and think that my nudity would offend. I am generally the only one to be clothed in Artwon. Naked is a standard way of life here."

With those words she stepped behind a fern partition and within moments was back in her leathers.

"Tell me what happened with the fringe?" I moved closer. "Can you leave with me now?"

Ria shook her head. "Thanks to your Brace, the fringe have mostly been disabled and I'm no longer worried about their presence here. But I have discussed with the clans. I just do not see how I can leave Artwon. There is no one to step in as an interim ruler and the packs very easily descend into chaos." She paused. "And there is still the issue of the other races of Regali trying to take over my territory."

"You do understand that if you don't help us the Seventine will be released and their plan is to destroy every world."

She regarded me with care. "I know that you believe this. I hear truth in your words, but the future is ever shifting and changing. The spirits have confirmed that there is a universal chaos, but they cannot see the final battle yet."

"Ria!"

Klea leapt into the doorway, her roaring words barely understandable. Unlike her usual half-woman half-lion visage, she was now a large tan lion creature with a short mane. Ria was at her side in seconds.

"What has happened?" She reached out to enclose the soft-looking paws in her hands.

Klea responded with lots of roaring yowls. They just sounded like animal noises to me, but clearly Ria understood. Her features paled; as she turned back to us she was chalky white.

"It is the sacred one; we must save her."

We were all on our feet, ready to go. I wondered who the sacred one was.

"There is no time to waste." Ria flung her hands skyward. "We must travel quickly and avoid the packs."

The room was suddenly flooded with light as the roof lifted up. I hadn't noticed that it was created from a series of overlaying tree branches. Vines descended in through the opening and threaded around our waists. I found myself flung up and dropped to land on top of Artwon's canopy. Somehow the dense canopy of the trees had flattened to form a path that we could travel on.

"Follow me," Ria yelled as she dashed across the path, looking like a flying fairy.

I was just about to move when a bright red globe caught my attention. This was the first time I'd seen the sky of Regali. The canopy was generally too thick, but standing there it felt like I was practically a part of the night and we were surrounded by seven large moons. They were massive, six blue and the largest of all was a red. Its beams of light cast the purple tint to the sky. They were one of the most mesmerizing things I'd ever seen.

"Abbs, come on. We can stare at the sky later," Lucy said as she dashed past me with Colton.

Brace stopped and waited for me. He knew we could catch up to them quickly.

"It's almost as beautiful as my house in the sky." I smiled at him.

There were no stars here, or I couldn't see them over the light of the moons. Stars would have made the picture perfect.

"Ready to go." I held out my hand to Brace.

He took it and then we were running, although it was fast enough to feel like flying.

We caught up to Colton and Lucy easily.

"Enjoying yourself, Luce?" I laughed as we broke even.

Colton had her arm and was dragging her along. I don't even think her feet touched the ground.

"Oh, yeah, loving it," she muttered. "My right arm was just for looks anyways. It had no practical use, so it's fine for dog-boy to dislocate it."

I could see Ria now. The moonlights reflected off the sheen of her hair. The jungle below us seemed to be alive, although there were fewer noises now.

"This is so awesome," I blurted. "It's as if we're running on top of the world."

"I feel so close to the sky." Lucy had her free arm out to the side, her face raised. "Like I could fly."

I let out a screech. "You are flying, Lucy."

It was true her feet were now far off the ground. Colton only had the barest hold of her hand. The moment I spoke she looked down.

"What the eff?" she stuttered, her eyes huge. She hit the ground hard then. "How did I do that?"

"I have no idea, Lucy, but it might be time to do some investigating into you." Colton was watching her closely. "There's no way you're an Earthling, not with your abilities."

"I agree," Brace said. "There's a strange energy inside you. I always thought it was your gift as a soothsayer, but there's something more."

"How could I be anything else?" She sounded confused. "I had parents. I was born in the adult compound."

I snorted. "That's what Olden told you. How old were you when you were left at the junior compound?"

"I was two," she said. "And you're right: I don't remember my life before that. I've only had Olden's word." Her face clouded over with anger. "Shame she was killed before I could torture her for answers."

Ahead of us, Ria slowed and then suddenly disappeared. My heart started to beat faster. Where had she gone?

When we reached the spot, I could for the first time see the edge of Artwon. It was a massive forest, spanning forever around us. As we slowed, the canopy opened and I gasped as vines shot forward and secured us again. We were lowered to the forest floor.

It took a few moments for my eyes to adjust to the dimmer light under the trees. But I felt them before I could see them; the Seventine were here.

Once my vision cleared the scene became alarmingly apparent. There were three men. They stood at the base of the largest tree I had ever seen. It was at least fifty feet across and rose up higher than I could see. It looked to sit above the canopy, and yet I hadn't seen it when we'd run across the branches.

Was this the sacred one Ria had referred to? The way she felt about nature, it would make sense. And if I focused I could feel a large thrum of energy vibrating through this tree.

"What is everyone freaking out about?" Lucy said in a low voice. "It's just three men."

"Three men possessed by the Seventine," Brace bit out.

If I zoomed in my eyesight to its full capabilities, I could see the fine cracking fissures on the men's skin. The power would not be contained for long, so right now we just needed to find out what they wanted.

"You must not harm the sacred tree." Ria strode forward until she was mere feet from them. "It is the lifeblood of Artwon."

"Oh, we know, Queen." I recognized the voice which came from the middle man. The first. "That's why it's our next energy tether. We did have a nice little gathered amount of power back on First World, but we understand that's no longer available, so we need a huge influx to free the fourth."

He must be talking about the room of horrors. I would have thought he'd be more visibly upset, but his tone was matter of fact.

"It houses the tree spirits," Ria cried.

And I remembered that was where her mother existed.

He laughed. "Even better."

At that point the three humans joined hands and faced toward the giant tree. Ria rushed at them but was thrown back, along with all the vegetation she was sending their way.

"Help me!" she screamed as we reached her side and Brace pulled her to her feet. "How can we stop them?"

I shook my head. "I told you the only way is to lock them back up. They're the original power; we have no way to stop this."

Suddenly the tethers of the sacred tree were now visible. And there looked to be thousands if not hundreds of thousands. It was old and it was powerful, and before my eyes the Seventines' power was cutting through the ties. At first I couldn't see any change in the ancient and sacred tree, but as the tethers disappeared it began to shimmer. And then the leaves were the first to go – they simply vanished – followed by the branches.

"Oh, my sacred gods." Ria dropped to her knees. "This cannot be happening."

It took them two minutes. Two minutes to completely undo a tree that was probably –

"A million years," Klea moaned. The leon was back in her other form and was crouched beside

Ria. I hadn't noticed how many of the pack surrounded us. "It has stood here for a million years and now it is gone."

And it was gone. Fading from our sight like mist in the sun. The first, housed in the body of a First Worlder, turned to face us.

"Time to free the fourth," he said.

The shells they wore exploded before us. It was nothing like the power of Que, but it still knocked almost everyone down.

Brace was on his feet. He reached down and pulled me up.

"We have to hurry, Red." He gripped my chin firmly before leaning down and kissing me soundly on the lips.

"Uh, what?" I stuttered as he pulled back; he'd said something right.

He gave me a heart-stopping grin. "I said we need to hurry and perform the ritual. Before they release the fourth."

Screams started behind me. I spun quickly, my eyes darting left and right to find the problem.

It was Ria.

She stood before the sacred tree space and as I moved to her side I noticed what had caused her anguish. It was barely discernible, but spanning out from the newly untethered sacred tree, slivers of brown threaded the vines.

"They're dying," she sobbed. Leaves and vines were wrapping themselves around her in comfort. "If the tree is not restored all of Artwon will die."

I reached out and, pushing through the foliage, found her hand and gripped it tight. "I don't know for sure, but our research indicates that if the Seventine are re-imprisoned all the tethers will be restored. So if you leave and help with the fourth ritual, it might be over today."

"And if the ritual does not work?" Her violet eyes bored into me.

"Then we have to beat them in the final battle." And I had to give up Brace and my very soul.

She turned away to stare at the faint signs of Artwon's death.

With a sigh she nodded. "Yes, I will join you. There is no point ruling only to let my world die around us." She raised her voice. "Packs, unite."

They moved from all over to circle around us.

"I am leaving to try and restore the sacred tree. I authorize Klea as interim leader, but she will confer with each pack elder on all decisions. Abby will bring me back as frequently as possible, so if you can wait to do anything major I will be around."

Noise exploded from the pack members. Klea's growls silenced them again.

"Yes." Ria started to answer their questions. "Artwon will die without the sacred tree. I would not leave if it wasn't this important. I promise I will do everything in my power to save our land."

She flicked her eyes up to lock on me. "We have no time to spare, right? I can't spend one last night giving Klea instructions."

I pursed my lips before shaking my head. "We have to perform the ritual before they release the fourth. It's our only chance."

She sighed, turning to Klea. "I'm sorry, old friend. But I trust you, and I know you will rule fairly and with compassion in my stead."

"I will try my best." Klea nodded her head toward her Queen. "Just hurry home. I am not a ruler; I do not have the temperament. You are the true Queen."

Ria pulled herself free from the plants to hug her friend.

"If I don't make it back, get them to safety," I heard her whisper. "Find somewhere else on Regali for them to live. Stay together as one strong unit."

Klea growled once as she pulled back. Ria then turned and, touching one finger to her brow, she seemed to salute the rest of the pack members. Everyone in the clearing dropped to their knees before her, a united sign of respect. Ria gave an audible swallow.

"Let's go," she said, her voice barely a whisper.

I didn't waste any time. I couldn't afford for her to change her mind.

I traced the five of us back to our house in Angelisian. I chose the front white room as our landing place and as soon as everyone started to move I used my power to sense who was around. There was a faint feeling of Talina's energy coming from the direction of the ocean, but that was all I could detect.

"Now what do we do? What is the next step to finding and destroying these Seventine?" Ria's voice was as hard as timber.

I figured it wasn't the time to remind her that we couldn't destroy them, only imprison them.

"I need the other half-Walkers: Talina from Spurn and Fury from Crais," I explained. "Then we go to the entrance of their prison to perform the ritual of the four."

She stared at me for an extended moment. And her expression said that I was doing too much talking and not enough moving.

"Alright then, I'll go get Fury. You all can wait to see if Talli surfaces." I threw Lucy a deadpan look.

She returned it with the slightest grin. Ria was not a happy camper.

I spun around and lifted my face in anticipation of Brace's kiss. He did not disappoint. It was brief, but so hot as he slipped his tongue between my parted lips I was practically panting when he pulled away.

"Shouldn't we get dinner if there's going to be a show?" Colton drawled.

Lucy laughed in one short burst. Those two were far too similar for my liking.

"Behave." I waved my hands at them. "I'll be back soon."

I traced my way straight to the room of horrors, but it was empty. Staring around the space I realized that now it was empty of the thousands of bodies it was absolutely massive. The walls appeared to be made of a reflective white surface and somehow light shone from tiny spaces along the joins. It was cold and sterile. But there was no time to examine the ins and outs. I needed to find Fury. I lowered the shields of my mind.

Dad, where are you? I called for Josian.

His presence filled my mind immediately. For some reason he never seemed to have a shield up. I'd ask him about that one day.

Aribella, nice to hear from you, baby girl. We're at the castle, in the throne room.

I'll be right there, I said as I reshielded myself.

I wasted no time tracing into a corner of the castle's throne room. My sudden appearance was unseen as the large area was filled with crying and screaming people, which I assumed were the awoken victims from the horror room.

"Hey, Abby, how is everything?"

I spun to face the person with the soft calm voice. It was Francesca.

"Crazy, isn't it?" She nodded to the hysteria. "Half of them are family and friends who thought their loves ones were lost."

I took a deep breath. "Are you okay? I'm sorry you ended up in that situation."

She gave a strangled laugh. I wished I could read more from her eyes, but as usual the pure white globes gave away nothing.

"Que found me, tried to turn me into his own personal oracle. He broke me down, built me up again and broke me again. I'd have done anything to make it stop, but my powers had other ideas. I haven't had a vision in months."

"So that's why he strung you up for your energy?"

She nodded. "Yes, he said I might as well be useful to him."

"Tell me about Samuel?" I said, my voice hardening. "Why did he betray us? And why did you never warn me that he was in with Que? Surely you saw something?"

"Why don't you just ask me yourself, Aribella?" Samuel said as he stepped out of the crowd with Lallielle and Josian right behind him.

"I never saw anything." Francesca's voice was a whisper. "My power has forsaken me." And with that she started to wail and sob.

I left Lallielle to comfort her while I faced Samuel.

"You have two seconds to speak or I'm going to break your nose again."

He laughed. It sounded harsh with his husky voice. His throat had been damaged during his imprisonment on Earth.

"I didn't betray anyone. Or I wasn't aware that I was," he said, and I fought the urge to roll my eyes. "At some point on Earth Que must have done something to me. He rolled my mind. When I returned to First World I was mostly in control of my actions, but occasionally I'd find myself waking up with missing time. I'd have eight or ten hours I couldn't account for."

His eyes implored me to believe him. But I didn't.

"Where's Lucy?" he finally asked after a few moments' silence.

"Stay away from her." I pointed my finger at him.

"You don't believe this, right?" I spun to face my silent father.

He shook his head, crossing his arms over his broad chest. "I'm reserving judgment. Que definitely had the energy levels for something like that, but it's also a mighty convenient excuse."

He leaned down close to my ear. "Your mother believes him, though. She's insisting he come home. But I'll be keeping a close eye on him."

I sighed. Of course my soft-hearted mother would be taken in by his con. He was her son and she'd never believed he could be so evil.

"Have you seen Fury?" I asked Josian, getting back to the most important part. "Ria's at our home. We're ready to perform the ritual."

"She said she wasn't breathing the same air as a punk-ass backstabber," Samuel said, overhearing my question. "I believe she and the red man went out into the courtyard."

I caught the slight grin on his lips.

I couldn't help my own grin as I turned away. That was so Fury.

"Contact me when you're back at the prison," Josian said. "I'll come and make sure nothing goes wrong."

"And be careful," Lallielle added over Francesca's shoulder.

"You got it." I blew them both a kiss.

I made my way through the masses of emotional people. I didn't feel any Walker power in the group, so I guessed they'd already left for other worlds.

As I passed by one expressive and stricken face after another I wondered if any of them would truly recover from this ordeal, or were there just some things too all-encompassing to come back from?

I thought of Lallielle's face when she'd talked of losing me and Samuel, and I knew there were definitely some things that would change you fundamentally. You could never be the same person again.

Chapter 12

I found that tiny courtyard without any more distractions. It was relatively unadorned, besides one thud tree in the center, its branches casting off spheres of shade in the sunlight. I strode out to stand beside the thick trunk, looking around. It took me a few moments to notice them. They were tucked into the corner, and they were very busy.

And then, right in the middle of their kissing session, Fury burst into flames. Dune threw his head back, her rejuvenating flame working on his energy levels immediately. It always amazed me the physical changes I could see when he absorbed the fire.

I waited until they were done, and as I watched them something occurred to me. Why didn't their clothes burn? I knew there was nothing special about them. They were just First-World fibers and should be flammable. But it was as if whatever touched their bodies didn't burn. That was odd and convenient.

"Are you just going to stand there like a weird creeper nomad?" Fury swung her head to grin at me as her flames disappeared.

I snorted. "An audience doesn't usually bother you ... don't tell me you're having performance issues." I raised one brow.

She laughed, strolling forward, her hand entwined with Dune's, their pure white hair glowing.

"You wish, supes."

She'd shortened Super Abby to 'supes'. Since she said it ten times a day, apparently her tongue was getting tired.

I wasted no time filling them in. "So Ria, the Regali half-Walker, is back at the house. We need to go right away and try this ritual. The Seventine were on Regali. They stole the energy from their oldest sacred tree, which gives them enough to free the fourth. So we have no time to waste. We have to beat them."

The carefree look fell from her face and warrior Fury was back.

"Alright then, take us to the beach house," she said, dragging Dune up to me.

I traced us into the front room. I never worried about anyone being in the space where I landed. Josian had explained that two objects cannot occupy the same space, so if I traced into a place then, according to the rules of the universe, there would be nothing in that spot. It would either have moved or I would land a little to one side of where I was aiming.

The front room was empty, but I could see everyone through the front window. They were out by the water, their backs to us as they faced the expanse of ocean.

Talli hasn't surfaced yet. Brace's warm tones echoed.

I smiled like a silly jerk. He made me so happy. Even when he was annoying me, he still made me happy.

You make me happy too. Now get that gorgeous butt out here so I can fill my arms. They're feeling a little empty.

You're also getting a little sappy in your old age, I teased as the three of us made our way out of the house and across the green grass.

When the sand hit my boots, I resisted the urge to reach down and take them off. There was no time to indulge in beach therapy right then.

Ria turned at the sound of us squeaking across the sand. Her eyes rested on Fury before coming back to me.

"Ria, this is Fury of Crais and her mate Dune," I said.

The girls exchanged a nodded greeting, but that was as far as it went.

"I wish I was visiting here under better circumstances," Ria said as she turned back to the ocean. "There is so much to explore. I never imagined that a body of water existed like this." Her purple eyes widened. "And it is undrinkable. What is the point of it then, and why are there no trees?"

She indicated toward Angelisian. And I understood what she was asking.

"People can't really live in trees here. They don't have the skills or power. So they build their homes on the ground." I sighed. "Unfortunately they need open space to do that so sometimes the environment suffers."

Ria's face hardened as I spoke.

"Luckily First World is really very conscious of their natural wonders," Lucy added. "You don't want to visit Earth. They've razed the rainforests to the ground."

Ria gasped. "My heart hurts," was all she said, and I couldn't blame her.

Unable to stay away any longer, I stepped over to Brace. It took all my willpower not to throw him to the ground and tear his clothes off.

"Damn willpower," he muttered as his long arms closed around me in a comforting and tingle-inducing hug.

I wished we had more time, but I had to beat the Seventine.

Since I was already on the edge of the ocean it was easy enough to throw out my energy toward the water, in a sort of dolphin call for Talina. I hoped she would recognize me and get her butt out. There was no way any of us could chase her under the sea.

We continued to wait.

Lucy sat back from the wet sand. Colton was near her and he – I had to look twice – he was building a sand castle. Or sand boobs, by the looks of those weird mounds.

"You have a dirty mind, Red. That's a mini map of our planet, Abernath, he was showing Lucy before." Brace grinned down at me.

I took a moment to look at it a little closer.

"So there are the seven main inhabited planets, but there are also lots of little worlds scattered around?" I asked. "Like Josian's place."

"Yes, there are many smaller globes that orbit around the pull of larger tethered worlds. Walkers mostly use these as home bases when they're not on the big seven."

I gave a brief chuckle. "I still almost can't believe the life I live now. I never knew any of this existed when I lived on Earth."

And with that thought two human-fish people surfaced at the back of the breaking waves. Case in point. Talina rose up with the crest of a swell and gave me a happy wave. My heart filled with pure joy for her. She was the kindest of souls and I hated that she'd lost everyone. I hoped that the reunion with Ladre went well.

"Oh, she looks so happy." Lucy had moved to stand beside me. She paused for an extended moment before speaking again. "So did you see Samuel before?"

My head spun round to meet her eyes. She looked calm, as if this were just a casual conversation. But her question had a sense of urgency.

"Yes," I said, "he told me a story about how his mind was possessed, he was losing track of time, didn't know what he was doing." I snorted. "A very lame attempt at explaining. He should just own his evil-ness."

Lucy's brow crinkled. "What if it's true? There just seemed to be so much for it all to have been an act."

I sighed. "Luce, I don't want you to get sucked back in. I don't even think there's enough good deeds in the world for Samuel to redeem himself."

Not only for what he'd done to Brace but also for how he'd hurt Lucy and Lallielle. They had both suffered from his actions.

"Abbs has too much warrior in her. We're not quick to forgive betrayal," Brace drawled as he watched our water-friends approach. "Even if Samuel was somehow a victim, his weakness cost everyone a lot."

Brace's words, whilst supportive, reminded me of something. My own weakness was the reason the third Seventine had been released. Who was I to judge anyone else's betrayal? Maybe Samuel deserved a chance to prove himself. All I could do was keep an eye on him and make sure he didn't hurt anyone else.

"You know what, you're right, Lucy. We should reserve judgment in case his story has some truth."

My drastic turn around had her shooting me a confused look, but all Brace did was shift his expression from stoic to a half-smile. I narrowed my eyes. Had he deliberately made that comment so I would let up on Samuel a little? Wouldn't put it past him, damn sneaky Walkers.

"I can do that," Lucy finally said.

"Lucky I'm here to stop all you tender-hearted souls from getting yourselves killed," Colton muttered as he stood next to Brace, their stances mirror images of each other.

Brace laughed but didn't comment again. I really had no idea what his feelings were about this situation. He was keeping it very close to his chest at the moment.

Talina was in the shallows now; she strode out, water running off her in rivulets. Her emerald-colored hair looked luscious and vibrant. It had enjoyed the swim.

"Where's Ladre?" I asked as she drew closer.

I could have sworn I'd seen him before.

"He's not quite ready to face everyone. He'll stay in the ocean." She smiled brightly.

Lucy and I groaned.

"You're going to be insufferably chipper and happy now, aren't you?" Lucy said in a mock-devastated voice.

Talina laughed, reiterating our points. "I am very happy," she said.

"Oh, you will be elaborating on that later." I gave her a pointed look.

"So what are we doing now? I assume you called me because I'm needed." Talina pushed her heavy locks behind her ears.

I pointed toward the stunning chestnut-haired Queen. "Talli, meet Ria of Regali. She's the fourth half-Walker. We're going now to perform the ritual."

Talina walked up to Ria. Unlike Fury, she was friendly and held out a hand.

"It's so nice to meet you," she said with a huge grin. "Welcome to the half-Walkers."

Ria just stared down at the offered hand for a moment before reaching out and tentatively touching it. With a smile Talina showed her how to shake hands and after a brief moment pulled away.

"Let us go now. I really do need to return to my people." Ria addressed me.

I could see the lines of stress around her eyes; she was worried. I really hoped this ritual worked, not just for her sake but for all of ours. And more personally so that I could avoid having to break my melding bond with Brace.

I wasn't comfortable tracing that many people, so Brace opened a doorway to the large room in the dark mountains. The one with all the tunnels off it. We started down number eight.

The mountains seemed quieter now. That evil energy which always tormented me there had abated. Brace held my hand as we walked. He was on high alert. I knew both of us were waiting for an ambush. The Seventine would be close by, preparing to release their fourth.

The light from the prison came into view, its bright sparkles filled with many colors.

"Can you feel them?" I said in a low voice to Brace.

He was more in tune with the Seventine than anyone else.

"They're around but not close at the moment." He pulled me closer to him. "But I wouldn't let my guard down."

He didn't have to worry. I was so tense I was practically vibrating as I walked.

We crossed over the doorway threshold into the prison room. The light was practically blinding this close. It was white again, but I knew it would turn red if the fourth was released.

"Alright, Abbs, what do we have to do?" Brace pulled me closer to the entrance.

"The Walker was a little light on details. But he said that we needed to combine the blood of four half-Walkers and as we sprinkle it into the prison we need to chant *invictius collasa repeta intombre.*" My memory was so good now I didn't even have to strain my thoughts to recall the words.

I repeated them a few times, and then the girls chimed in. When I felt they had the wording perfect, I pulled my knife from my boot. This damn thing was coming in handy for these rituals.

"Why does it always involve bloodletting?" I heard Lucy sigh. "It's so unoriginal. Now if we had to bring flowers and plant them, that would be different. Or release butterflies."

Colton laughed. "Blood is powerful and it's what gives us life. In our veins our power runs. Blood binds them to the prison. It makes sense it would be needed to re-entomb them." He raised his brows at her. "Besides, if you want something, you need to give something back."

"The great balance," Ria said.

"Thank you, Colton – smart-ass," Lucy muttered.

Colton laughed again, shaking his head this time.

The opening was too large for us half-Walkers to stand right around and hold hands, so we stood close on one side. I held up my right hand.

"Are we all ready?" I asked.

I could see a few nerves, but everyone just nodded and held one hand out toward me. My knife was sharp enough for this job. I was pretty nuts about making sure my weapon was well cared for. Having a blunt knife could end up being a fatal mistake.

And that made it easy to press down on the fleshy pad of each hand for a clean cut. I didn't wipe it off in between. We couldn't contract blood-borne diseases, so there was no point worrying about cross contamination. Plus in the end we had to press all of our hands together.

As soon as we were bleeding all over the floor we linked our bloodied hands together and, holding them out over the entrance, I started to chant. The girls quickly joined in.

"Invictius collasa repeta intombre. Invictius collasa repeta intombre. Invictius collasa repeta intombre."

We repeated it three times just to be safe. I watched the last of our blood rain down into the opening as the wounds healed. And I waited to see what would happen.

In that moment of pause, from the shadows flew three golden spirits.

"It's the Seventine," Brace said, and without hesitation he threw out a shield around us.

They started to circle, and it took a few minutes before I realized something was hurting my ears. They were making a noise. It was uncomfortably high pitched and increasing in frequency as they spun.

"They're speaking," Brace said as he turned, keeping them in sight. "You need to use your ears to slow and lower the noise."

"Oh, right," Fury said, "because all of us can just use our ears for that."

"What are they saying?" I asked Brace.

He didn't answer straight away. His eyes flicked around as he continued to follow their movement.

"They're freeing the fourth," he finally bit out.

My head dropped; our ritual hadn't worked.

"Let's try it again." Ria grabbed my hand. "Maybe we didn't do it long enough."

I stared at her for an extended moment before nodding. I still held the knife so within seconds I cut into our palms again. Ignoring the sting, I held out my hand with the other half-Walker girls. Together we started to chant.

The Seventine were still circling us, their own high-pitched noise mingling with our chanting. I could feel something then. It was as if our two energies or rituals were battling against each other.

"They're feeding energy into the prison walls," Brace yelled. "There's too much; you're not strong enough."

Screw that. I was not letting them free another one.

I threw out my tethers, connecting to each of the girls and bringing their power to life. I could feel Ria's shock; I'd forgotten that she had no idea I could do this. Her power added another dimension, a real earthy feel to the fire and water. Fury was covered in her flames, a watery whirlpool surrounded Talina, and ivy sprung from Ria. I almost couldn't believe it, but I was sure it came from her hair.

"That is incredible," I heard Lucy say.

"Remind me not to piss Red off either," Colton said. "She's as lethal as Brace. Gods help us if they have little ones."

For some reason I liked being thought of as badass like Brace. I met his eyes and his returning smile was as panty-dropping as I'd ever seen. Damn, he rocked sexy like nobody's business. I forced myself to turn away, back to the prison. This was my last chance to save my melding bond. A bond I wasn't sure I could survive without.

We were still chanting loudly. I started to feed our combined powers into the prison walls, my intent to strengthen the bonds. The Seventines' screeching was still increasing in tempo and frequency; if that continued my ears were going to start bleeding.

I saw Lucy stumble to the ground, her hands covering her ears. I was about to panic but Brace knelt beside her and placed his hands on either side of her face. Her relief was apparent.

It's not working. Ria's voice sounded desperate.

Don't give up, I encouraged her.

Her head snapped around to stare at me. She also hadn't known we could hear her.

We can all communicate when Abby tethers to us, Talina said. *She increases our power.*

Okay, Ria said, *so what else can we do right now to stop this?*

I wished I had an answer for her, but I didn't know what else we could do together. There'd been no time to find out.

I've been practicing and despite the fact I can't control the power when Abby is tethered to us, I can direct more energy into her, Fury said in rapid succession. *Pour all your power into her and she can send it out.*

Finally something I knew how to do. I'd taken a lot of Fury and Talina's power the last time we'd tried this, but add in another half-Walker and the increased level was incredible. It felt like far more than just one extra.

The build-up hit me hard and fast. I could feel the girls weakening as I drained their energy, and just as the golden cords tethering us started to fray I released all of that build-up into the prison.

Lights exploded and what felt like fireworks ricocheted around the stone room. The screeching of the Seventines stopped. Like they had been cut off mid-bellow.

The girls collapsed around me, exhaustion wracking their features. And after expelling everything from inside I too found my legs too weak to hold me.

Brace was at my side. He threw me over one shoulder and Talina over the other. From my precarious position I noticed Colton grab Ria and Dune gently cradle his Fury, and then the men, followed by Lucy, zoomed out of the mountain.

I was disorientated from my lack of energy, so it took me a few moments to figure out why all the rush.

Then I noticed the red light splashed along the rock surfaces as we exited. We might have expelled the Seventine, but we'd failed to stop the fourth releasing.

I lifted my head to examine the determined planes of my mate's features as he ran. He was so focused on getting us to safety he didn't notice my examination. Tears pricked my eyes and ran down my cheeks.

I was going to lose him.

Lucy, who was just behind, running as fast as her little legs could carry her, caught my eyes. Her face fell too. She blinked rapidly a few times, her expression a mixture of sympathy and pain. I had to bury my face in Brace's shoulders or I was going to sob my heart out like a baby.

When we reached the outside, the sooty ash of the dead land rose around us. Brace opened a doorway and everyone filed through. We exited onto the grassed area in front of my house. I was thankful again that the Angelisian beach house was private and slightly isolated. Although our neighbors were used to strange happenings here, it was pretty common knowledge that Walkers were drama magnets.

"What happened?" Ria threw herself off Colton's shoulder. She was still weak, stumbling. "Why did it not work?"

As she lay half collapsed on the ground, tendrils of grass started to rise and wrap around her legs. Damn, she had an awesome power.

I rubbed my temples. A headache was starting a low pound at the base of my skull. Brace lowered Talina down first. She sank into the lush grass. I sat next to her.

"I don't know why it didn't work. It was never a sure thing." It's not like anyone had tried the ritual before. It was just legend handed down by the originals.

"So I can't go back to Artwon yet." Ria's voice was barely a whisper.

"I think it's because the Seventine were releasing the fourth at the same time." Brace looked grave. I wasn't sure I'd seen his face this coldly chiseled before. "The two energies collided."

"It definitely looked as if the fourth was released," Lucy said.

We locked eyes again in a silent communication.

I squeezed my eyes closed so tight that they ached. I knew what I had to do now, but was I strong enough? And how could I go through this without sharing the secret with Brace?

Chapter 13

Josian was pissed off.

I'd totally forgotten to bring him to the mountain and only remembered when I'd tried to contact him and find out when he'd be back. Lucy and I had decided we were going to need additional help. I had no idea how to break a melding bond. I was sure there had to be way – there was always something – but if there wasn't, this life was over for everyone. Josian had coldly informed me that he was on his way home now, and that I was going to get my ass kicked.

I'd happily sent Brace and Colton off to Abernath. They needed to go deal with the clan problems. And I needed a chance to gather information on how to break the bond.

"I'll be back for you soon. We need a night in the snow," Brace had promised me when he'd kissed me goodbye.

I wondered if that would be my last kiss for a while.

Ria, Talina and Fury were hanging out by the ocean. Through the front window I could see the three of them splashing in the shallows. Ria was handling her worry and disappointment a little better now, but I could see a glint of desperation in her gaze.

I was so feeling that today. Lucy was with me in the front room. We were just silent, staring out the window at the girls. I was wondering when they'd had it repaired after I'd smashed through it.

"I think the vision was wrong." Lucy interrupted my musing. "I've barely had a prophecy since the gathering. It's as if something was prompting them."

I snorted unhappily. "Can we really risk it?"

"I need to speak with Frannie." Lucy rested her chin on her hand. "She might be able to shed some light on my messed-up version of being a soothsayer."

Since Francesca's visions had also dried up I wondered if she would be any help.

A doorway opened behind me. Josian's power stormed through in a mass of energy that had my hair standing on end and my heart-rate increasing. He was followed by an unsmiling Lallielle, freaky white-haired Francesca and lastly Samuel.

I heard Lucy's soft gasp.

I should have warned her that he would be coming. I knew that my parents would be keeping a close eye on him for a long time. He would have to earn their trust back.

I prepared for my father's angry words. I deserved them. Instead, he enclosed me in a tight hug.

"You're trying your best to kill me. I'm not used to being stressed and now it's all I do. My daily thoughts consist of: what's Aribella doing right now? Have the Seventine hurt her? Do I have an ulcer?" He pulled back to look at me. "And I know I found a gray hair this time."

I tried not to smile too broadly. "I'm so sorry. I got caught up in the ritual and … I forgot to call you. Where's Quarn?" He hadn't come through the doorway.

Lallielle laughed. I was so happy to see that. "Our daughter is just the same headstrong Walker personality as you, Josian. And Quarn is still at the castle, helping to sort out everything."

"Mom, can you show me which room you're moving me to?" Samuel interrupted. "After a few months of being a hanging energy bag … well, some new clothes wouldn't go astray."

"I second that thought," Francesca added.

Lallielle nodded, giving Josian a brief kiss as she moved toward the doorway. The entire time Samuel had been standing there he'd just stared at Lucy, and she'd steadfastly kept her eyes on the floor. It wasn't until he left that she looked up.

"Does he really have to stay here?" she asked out loud.

Josian's face hardened, his bronze eyes flashing. "I've tried to reason with Lallielle, but she insists that it's better he stay where we can keep an eye on him. I agree, but for different reasons to her."

If Lucy's face was anything to judge by, she was moving out today and sleeping on the beach.

"Lucky we aren't here much," I said.

"Any time is too much time." She sighed.

It was strange how Lucy seemed to alternate between hating him and feeling sorry for him.

"What did you need to talk to me about?" Josian interrupted.

I took a deep breath and caught Lucy's eye. This was her time to jump in.

"I had a vision, Jos," she started. "And it doesn't look good."

Josian sat silently while Lucy told her story. His expression didn't change, although his eye color shifted often between bronze, gold and amber.

"So right now I need to know," I chimed in when Lucy had finished explaining, "is there any way to break a melding bond?"

Sympathy laced his expression as he faced me. "You do know what you're asking? To break the melding bond is akin to me tearing your heart from your chest." He laughed. "Actually, it's worse than that, because you won't die, but you'll wish you had."

I nodded. "It's the last thing I want to happen. I can barely breathe when Brace is just off on Abernath world doing his Princeps thing. But we're talking about the fate of every living thing on seven or more worlds."

Josian nodded. "I know: there's no choice, but I just wanted to prepare you for how bad it's really going to be."

I gulped. "So there is a way? And do you agree with Lucy that I shouldn't tell Brace?" I think I'd been secretly hoping it was impossible.

He nodded. "Despite the fact no one has seen a melding bond since the beginning of our time, I have an idea that might work. And if you tell Brace, he'll never let you break the bond. I would kill for Lallielle. Walker men never see reason

245

when it comes to their mates." His smile was sad. "When do you want to do this?"

Tears pricked my eyes at the thought. "As soon as possible, I guess. But I need a few days with Brace first. Then, after I break the bond, once I pull myself together, I'll head to the next planet."

Josian met my gaze. "If you pull yourself together," he finished ominously.

I sucked in sharply. Damn, I hoped I was strong enough for this. "I'll meet you back here in a couple of days. And can you make sure I don't waver in my resolve?" I took my father's hand. "I need you to be strong if I can't."

He nodded, hauling me forward for a kiss on the cheek. "Your mother is planning on organizing a fair to celebrate the return of our people. Angelisian hasn't had one for many years. It'll be spectacular. You don't want to miss it. We can leave straight after that."

A smile crossed my face. I remembered Brace telling us about the town fairs when we first came here. It would be a great opportunity to see the different gifts of the First Worlders since they often had displays and shows.

Josian left the room after promising to explain to Lallielle and the girls where I'd gone for a few days. I hoped they would think I just needed time with Brace before going to the next world. No one could know of the vision. I needed them to keep the faith that we could beat the Seventine and, more importantly, Brace couldn't find out. Apparently he would lock me up and throw away the key.

"Can I please come with you?" Lucy turned her pleading blue eyes on me. "I know you want alone time and I'll stay out of your way, but I just can't be in the same house as Sammy yet. I'm not ready for that first conversation."

I hugged her. "Of course, Luce, you don't even have to ask."

How's everything going? I kept my tone light as I contacted Brace.

Missing you like crazy. I can't get away for a few days, so let's decide now when we'll be together again.

I mentally pictured his strong jaw and chocolate eyes. The sound of his voice was like coming home. I couldn't believe I was going to lose that.

Funny you mention that, how about Lucy and I visit for a few days before I head to the next planet? I'd like to see Abernath world.

His tone lightened as he answered. *Sounds like the best idea ever, but are you sure you can waste any time before heading to the next planet?*

Right now there was nothing more important than what was going to happen.

Lallielle is having a celebratory town fair in Angelisian in a few days. I really want to see that, so I figured I could go to the next world when it's over.

I'll be there in a few minutes for you and Lucy. You don't need anything. Our home here is very well equipped for visitors.

My heart fissured a little more at the words 'our home'.

See you soon, love, he said as he withdrew from my mind.

Lucy was waiting patiently. She always knew when I was physically but not mentally present.

"All good?" she asked.

I nodded. "Yep, he's on his way now. Apparently we don't need anything."

"Yeah, sure, they always say that, forgetting my legs don't go on for miles."

"Word," I said with a laugh, "you're single-handedly bringing back the rolled-up pants look."

"No, I'm not." She sniffed. "Should be a punishable offence to wear that bad a fashion statement."

She rubbed her head then, her eyes closing. My heart stilled. Was she having a vision? I was starting to dread the bad news her gift brought. Finally her lids popped open again, her hand still holding her head.

"I might not be getting many, but when they do come the visions are a little quicker and easier now," she said, dropping her hand. "The longer I fight it the worse it is when it comes."

"What did you see?" I bit out in my impatience.

"Oh, right." She laughed. "Nothing too crazy. We were with Brace, standing somewhere with very green grassed mountains, and for some reason you were lying flat on the ground." Her nose screwed up a little. "Pretty strange vision, if you ask me. I'm not sure what the point was."

I shrugged. Couldn't have been too important if that was all she'd got.

A doorway opened in the corner of the room and Brace's power entered before he did. It was as if he had a circumference of energy around him at all times.

His strong features softened as he met my gaze. Like a magnet drawn to its polar opposite, I couldn't stop my feet from crossing the room and entering his embrace. My feet left the ground as he pulled me into his arms and up to meet his hard chest.

"Hello, precious." He kissed my lips, pressing down hard and capturing me completely.

"Get a room," Lucy trilled as she moved closer.

I laughed, pulling back a little.

"You two should stop rubbing in my lack of a love life," she groaned.

Brace set me down so I was able to give her a gentle nudge. "I forgot that everything was about you."

"How could you forget that?" she asked. "I remind you at least once a day."

She wasn't kidding.

"Ready?" Brace moved toward the door, his hand entwined with mine as he pulled me along. "I was in the middle of a training session and need to get back."

"Ready as we'll ever be," Lucy said.

I found myself unable to answer. The faster time moved the closer I was to breaking the bond. I was never going to be ready for that.

We stepped into the doorway. I had one hand linked with Brace's and the other helped Lucy along, although we were using the doorways so much she was getting very good at negotiating the vacuum walk.

It was a fair distance along; these worlds must be far apart.

I was seeing lots of green at the other end. It was brightly lit, streaming light shining through the door. When we reached the end, Brace didn't hesitate, stepping through and bringing us with him.

All I saw as I stepped out onto the brightest green grass I'd ever experienced, was similarly shaded mountains in the background, and then, as if a ton had been dropped on me, I hit the ground.

Lucy let out a shriek. I tried to lift my head to see what had happened, but I couldn't move it off the ground. I also couldn't speak and my heart-rate was doing something strange.

"Abby, hang on, baby. I forgot about the gravity. Abernath has more gravity than any of the First World planets. We're in another star-system."

I could understand his words although my ears were having trouble adjusting. I might have missed some of what he said.

"I'll help Lucy with a little bit of shielding energy, but your Walker side will adjust for you in a moment."

He had barely said that sentence when I felt my body ease slightly. The pain and pressure in my chest and along my joints lessened, and I could move my head a fraction of an inch. Another few minutes and I was able to lift it off the ground. Breathing was easier and my heart stopped trying to pump itself out of my chest.

"I'm so sorry," Brace said again as he fitted his hands under my arm-pits and helped me up to a sitting position. "I just wanted you to see my world so badly. I didn't even take into consideration the differences which would affect you."

His expression was crestfallen. I could see how bad he felt.

"It's okay." The tightness in my throat eased. My voice sounded huskier. "No wonder you're so quick and fight like a ninja."

Relief crossed his face as I spoke. He helped me stand.

"Yes, when I move to a world with lighter gravity it feels as if I can float."

Training in this gravity would be beneficial, increasing my speed on First World by so much. I'd see if we could fit in a session before I had to leave. Who knew if I would get back again before the end of my journey?

Lucy was standing on my other side. She was looking around and appeared to be in no discomfort. I could see energy surrounding her, like a full-body force-field.

"Well, this was my vision," she said, indicating toward the mountains. "I guess I was supposed to be warned about the gravity."

I laughed. "Great warning."

"Yeah, it's a gift."

I took a moment to observe our surroundings. We were on the edge of what looked like a field.

And everything was a vibrant green, the grass and mountains running into each other. The only thing to break the endless color was a few scattered trees and a stream running in the shadow of the closest mountain. It looked almost unreal; like a painting.

"This is as close as we can get to the main compound via doorway. Que warded it many years ago against unauthorized entry," Brace said. "And the entrance is hidden."

He wasn't kidding. I could see nothing beyond the green sloping grass and large mountains. Brace started to move in the direction of the stream. Lucy followed without effort. I took a tentative step. My limbs and joints ached slightly, and I felt more tired and weighed down than usual, but managed to keep pace. But I definitely wasn't going to be running any marathons. At this thought I found my feet swept out from under me. Brace swung me into his arm, cradling me close.

"Your body will continue to adjust," he said. "Walkers can live anywhere."

When we reached the stream he barely broke pace, reaching down, and I think my eyes almost fell out of my head when he lifted the edge of the water like a large piece of paper and peeled it back. On the other side was a whole other world.

"Welcome to the Abernath world," Brace said as he ducked his head and stepped through.

He set me back on my feet, and I realized most of the discomfort had eased. It was almost like normal now for me to walk.

The noise hit me first. It had been silent on the other side but here a plethora of sounds abounded. It was a city. Huge, with a mix of old-fashioned and very advanced-looking modern facilities.

"This is where the majority of Abernaths reside; about ten thousand," Brace started to explain as we walked along the large main path. "Que decided long ago we were stronger together and, even though Walkers don't have a home planet, he searched until he found something suitable."

Faces turned as we ventured further into the bustling city. Men, women and for the first time Walker children. They had bright, curious faces, less innocent than Earth babies' but nowhere near as jaded as the adults that surrounded them protectively.

"Bwacie. Bwacie."

We stopped at the sound of a tiny voice screaming for Brace. A little girl burst into view, sprinting around a large group of women standing in front of a clothing store. I wasn't great at determining the age of children, but she looked about two. Her hair was raven black, hanging in silken waves down her back. Her skin was fair and her eyes were the same blue shade as –

"Colton." Lucy breathed out in a huff. "She looks just like Colt."

"Yes." Brace nodded as the little girl reached our side and he scooped her up. "This is Petal, Colt's niece."

"Magenta has a child?" I couldn't keep the shock from my face. She wasn't exactly the maternal type.

"No, not Magenta." Brace grinned at me; he'd read my thoughts.

"My mommy is missing, but she come back one day." Petal's voice was sweet as she snuggled into Brace's chest.

I was getting a strange range of emotions watching Brace cradle Petal so gently. It was clear that he loved her. Those damn tears pricked at my eyes again. It wasn't as if I wanted children any time soon, but one day I could picture Brace cradling our child just as lovingly. But who knew if that could ever happen now? I doubted my ability to destroy the Seventine. And I wasn't sure I believed that a melding bond could ever be restored after being broken.

Brace, who hadn't noticed my pain yet, continued to talk. "I never even knew she'd been born. I was on First World, but we've become friends, haven't we?" He tickled her little belly.

She giggled. The sound was infectious. "Love Bwacie."

Colton suddenly sprinted into view. The relief that crossed his face was apparent as he noticed Petal in Brace's arms.

"Dammit, kid, you're going to give me a heart attack," he said as he reached our side.

"You'd think they'd have learned by now not to leave you with any living thing to take care of." Brace laughed, handing the little girl across to her uncle.

She was so cute, refusing to let him go until he had given her three kisses.

"Five minutes. I was only watching her for five minutes and she was gone." Colton jiggled the little girl closer to him.

She snuggled into his shoulder, her eyes closing.

"I'll be right back," he said, before disappearing into the crowd.

We continued to walk along the path. Still no one had approached us, although most of the curious onlookers did give Brace a nod of respect as he passed them by.

"This is a small planet, about a thousand miles in circumference, but we only have the one city. Everyone lives here." He pointed out different landmarks.

The city looked pretty big. I could tell that we were only getting a brief glimpse. The houses and shops were similar to those I'd seen on Earth but made from strange materials.

We rounded a corner and suddenly this estate rose up before us. There were no gates or barriers that I'd noted so far, but it looked like this place should have huge security fences. It was spectacular, in that manicured, movie-star home way. A long path that was bordered by greenery on both sides led up to a two-story, cream-colored and old-manor-looking home. The framing was dark, contrasting nicely with the cream walls, and there were flowering vines climbing their way up strategically placed trestles.

Brace paused at the beginning of the path. "This is our Abernath home," he said to me.

"It's so lovely." I faced him. "Please don't tell me this was where Que lived."

Brace laughed. "No, this was my mother's family home. She gave it to me to raise my own family one day. Que lived over there."

He pointed to our left side and I turned my head to find an ugly monstrosity sitting on the top of a sloping hill. It was all steel, glass and metal. Cold and rising at least four stories into the air. And it was exactly where I would have expected Que to live.

"I hate that place. I closed it down the moment I got back and haven't stepped foot in it since." He stared at it for a moment, his expression hard, before he shook his head and faced me again. "Let's go inside so you can check the place out."

I smiled up at him. I couldn't wait to see if the inside was a beautiful as the outside.

"Colton's on his way," Lucy said, halting us before we moved again.

And indeed he was. He dashed up to where we stood at the start of Brace's beautiful home.

"Hello, Red, sorry I didn't have time to greet you properly." He swept me up in a hug, laying a solid kiss on my cheek. "You look stunning. Great to see you're here adding some class to Abernath."

I laughed. "You old charmer you."

He set me down and turned to Lucy.

"Hey, pretty girl." His voice lowered.

He leaned down to kiss her as well, but unlike mine, which was high on my cheek, hers landed close to the corner of her lips.

Lucy's face flushed and for once no smart comment emerged.

"Come," Brace interrupted. "Let's take our stage show inside for now."

I knew what he meant. We were the main attraction on the street right then. I'd thought the Walker gathering was bad, but this was ridiculous.

Inside, the house was perfect. I could see the women's touch, from the pastel colors to the delicate furnishings. But still Brace had added his own persona. There was a wicked weapons room downstairs, and his bedroom – well, our bedroom – was dominated by a massive bed. Definitely custom made, way beyond a king size. Princeps size maybe.

Colton and Lucy followed us around for the tour. They were being surprisingly formal and polite with each other, but I knew that couldn't last long.

Just as we settled into the kitchen, perched on high bench chairs, Magenta and another female walked into Brace's house. I might have bristled a little internally at the way Magenta so casually entered. No knocking or anything, as if she owned the place.

Lucy, on the other hand, was doing none of her bristling internally. She literally hissed like an angry cat. Especially when the other woman, a strawberry blond – who Colton greeted as Chelsea – laid a full on kiss on the blond wolf shifter. No wonder Lucy was in her fighting stance.

Colton pushed the clingy Chelsea away.

"Play nice, Chels, or I'll put you outside." Colton's tone was light but there was an edge to it.

He reached out and pulled Lucy to his side.

"This is Mag's best friend Chelsea." He introduced the pouty female.

She had golden eyes, almost the same shade as her hair, and was tall and willowy. Like most Walkers.

"This is Abby, Brace's mate, and Lucy. They're honored guests. Treat them with respect."

Brace hadn't said anything, but one look at his face had the two women lowering their heads deferentially. We didn't need any man to protect us, but that didn't mean it wasn't still nice.

"They need you in the training hall." Magenta addressed Brace. "There's been an incident."

He nodded. "Let them know I'll be there in a minute. And that I'm bringing my mate."

As he said the last statement I got the feeling the news was not going to go down well.

The two biatches (as Lucy called them) left us and we hurried to make a few sandwiches to take with us. I was starving.

"We need to move it," Colton said as we left, food clutched in our hands. "Abernaths can destroy shit faster than you can blink."

We hurried along a different path to the one we had come in on. There looked to be one sun-type ball in the air here. It was warm, the sky the color of rich cheese; a strong yellow.

Heading east from Brace's home, the road curved around and out of the main residential area. In these outer areas there was more space and the buildings seemed a little older. I could see a large warehouse in the distance. It wasn't actually until we came up to the side of it that its true size dawned on me. It was massive.

"This is the training facility for Abernath. Que demanded a minimum of three hours' training each day from the men," Brace said, leading us to the large double front door.

"What about the women?" I asked, shoving the last of my sandwich in my mouth. I was too hungry to be elegant.

"Women were encouraged to train, but he was too old-school to demand it." Brace laughed. "And despite this my mother was one of the best Abernath fighters." He kissed me on the nose. "You would have liked her. You're alike in more ways than the ability to kick ass."

I knew that Brace's missing mother and sister played on his mind a lot. I wondered if we would ever find out what had happened to them.

As the double doors opened silence descended over the large room. A thousand men faced us, and in unison they hit the deck, down on one knee, faces bowed to Brace. My mate shook his head as he stepped further into the room, right up to the front of the first line formation.

"Rise." He projected his voice into a command. "I have told you repeatedly, I do not expect you to kneel every time I walk in the room."

Unlike his egomaniacal father.

It looked as if Brace had his work cut out to change the rituals their last Princeps had demanded for thousands of years. No wonder Brace had chosen to avoid Que and take the First World task of waiting for me. I'd have done anything to escape also.

Chapter 14

They were like robots: highly trained, expressionless, and unable to think for themselves. They stood in formation, twenty across and hundreds deep.

"I've canceled mandatory training, but none of them know what to do each day. So they just end up back here," Brace said as we observed them.

The Walker men looked nothing alike. There were all varieties of hair, skin and eye colors – many of which I'd never seen on a person before – and yet they were all the same.

"How did Colton end up as such a smart-ass?" Lucy asked. "Que seems to have knocked the personality out of every male Abernath."

Colton gave a snort of laughter. "Seriously? You're calling me a smart-ass." He shook his head.

"Colt's wolf protects him from the worst of Que's brainwashing. No one owns the wolf." Brace sighed. "And most of these men are almost normal when they're outside the training hall. They have families and interact. But it was inside these walls that a lack of discipline was punishable."

He rubbed his arm then. I knew the slight and all but invisible marks littering his body were from Que.

"So what's the issue that Magenta was going on about?" I couldn't see anything out of the ordinary. Or whatever was deemed ordinary on Abernath.

At these words the men parted down the center. There was a raised platform in the middle of the room. On it was a single ornate chair, and next to that was a stool. Brace stopped, his expression freezing.

"What is it?" I asked.

"They want me to officially take the chair as Princeps," he bit out. His eyes darkened. "I think they're worried I'll refuse in the end."

I laughed. "Doesn't sound like they're too downtrodden. Get your butt up there and take your mantel, Princeps Brace." I gave him a gentle shove.

He captured my hand and started pulling me along with him.

"What are you doing?" I tried to pull myself free.

"I'm nothing without you," he said, his warm tones washing over me. "We do this together or not at all."

I wanted to refuse. In fact I wanted to run screaming from the room because I wouldn't be there for Brace. I was going to break his heart and my own. But there was no other choice. It was me who had made the decision to free the third Seventine, and now I needed to do everything in my power to make sure we didn't destroy the worlds.

I dragged my feet a little but in the end I did nothing; I let him pull me to the platform. We stepped up, thousands of faces turning in our direction. At some point others had entered and were immersed amongst the men. Women, children ... I would guess every Abernath was now there.

Brace sat on the chair and pulled me onto his lap. I was pretty sure the stool had been for me, but he was having none of that. The platform started to lift us into the air.

"What's going to happen?" I whispered to him.

"It's very simple. Just an absorbance of our people's power."

We were now level with the taller heads surrounding us. I could see no mechanism that was lifting us, but still we continued to rise.

"Does it matter that I'm not an Abernath?" I wondered how a cross-mating like ours worked.

"That's the reason for the power. You'll take some of Abernath into your energy and we'll recognize that you're one of us for all time."

This was going to backfire on me for sure.

Once the platform reached a few feet above everyone, it halted. The Abernaths each dropped to one knee, a fisted hand clenched over their chests.

"Princeps," they chanted as one. "We command."

More words were stated, but they weren't in English so I had no idea what they meant.

"Prepare yourself," he murmured in my ear.

I was about to ask what he was talking about when the energy hit me. In unison every Abernath sent power into us. Spreading around the room, it ricocheted out until it hit the center and Brace and I were the eye of its focus.

If I hadn't been cradled in his strong arms I would have hit the deck. The power slammed into me, and then, as if searching for my inner crevices, it seeped into my being, my soul, and somehow everything that I was started to morph inside. My eyes shifted to lock on Brace's. His marks were glowing, the blacked interspersed with other shades of gray, purple and gold.

"The colors will fade," he said, his warm expression locking me in. "You should see your marks right now."

I looked down at my arm and almost shrieked. My blood-red lace had the same shades running throughout. And our marks were intermingling again, the ends reaching out to each other and joining. I could feel our melding bond, and now I could also feel a new bond, my one to the people of Abernath.

"What's it like for you?" I asked in awe.

It was as if I could sense a small part of every person there.

See for yourself.

He pulled me inside his head. And I was immersed in everything that was Brace. My slight feeling for each person was increased a million inside him. His sense of responsibility was huge. He cared for every person; he worried for them and wanted to correct the wrongs of his father.

We'll always know our people. If any Abernath energy comes near us, we'll feel it. I know you have your mission right now, but once we've destroyed the threat of the Seventine, we can have any life we choose.

I couldn't stop myself from kissing him then. I slammed my lips down onto his soft mouth, not caring that thousands stared at us. I was lost in the moment, and it was only as I returned to reality that I realized that cheers and applause rang out through their training building.

I finally caught sight of Lucy. She was still standing near the doorway. Her worried expression met mine over the cheering heads, and I knew she was thinking the same thing as me: I was in trouble.

It took a long time for Brace to escape from the training hall. I was introduced to more Abernaths than I would ever remember. They greeted me with the weird forearm handshake of the Walkers. By the fiftieth time I had it down like a pro. Finally we made it back to his house. The four of us stood there in the front sitting room, just staring at each other.

"Well, that was unexpected," Colton finally said. "I assume no one told me because I would have definitely given you the heads-up."

Brace laughed. "I don't know, Colt. You can keep secrets in the right situation."

Lucy's head swung up then, her expression intrigued.

"Do tell." She smiled in her sweet manner. "What secrets is young Colton keeping?"

"I am at least five hundred years older than you," he huffed. "And I have no secrets that are worth sharing."

"I disagree," Lucy said. "You have at least one that influences the decisions you make."

He stared at her for a long moment. His white-blue eyes shifted to me. "Can you spare Lucy for a few hours? There's something I want to show her."

"Hello," Lucy interrupted me before I could speak. "Standing right here and able to make up my own mind about whether I am free or not. And I am not."

She emphasized the last words strongly.

Colton reached out and took her hand. "Please, I think once you see this you'll understand me better."

Her expression softened. She pursed her lips for a moment before giving a swift nod. Then without another word the pair walked out the door. Colton's massive height dwarfed her completely, but unlike with Samuel, they seemed to fit together. I hadn't noticed before. Even though Colton always lingered protectively over her, he didn't crowd down on her making her seem small. Unlike Samuel.

"Don't worry about us, guys," I called as the door slammed shut. "Thanks for all the concern, but Brace and I will find something to occupy ourselves."

I turned to face him. "Gee, you'd think they'd forgotten we …" My words trailed off as I caught sight of his expression.

My pulse skyrocketed and I think I stopped breathing. If I could have bottled the pure devastatingly sexy aura Brace was emitting right then I would have made millions on Earth. I was afraid to break the moment. The energy running between us was practically visible. It was potent and hot and … holy hell … I sucked in a ragged breath, but before I got to take a second he had me in his arms. We just barely made it to his room. And I finally figured out the advantages of his massive bed.

It took half the afternoon but finally when the urgency and passion had eased a little between us I had a minute to catch my breath. Right then I couldn't find it within myself to regret that moment, despite the pain that I was sure to experience when the bond broke.

"What are you thinking, Red?" Brace's husky tones sent shivers along my body, or it might have been the way he continued to run the pads of his fingertips over my naked skin. "I shouldn't have to even ask you that, but since you insist on keeping me locked out of your mind ..."

I could hear the unasked question there. He didn't understand why I wouldn't want him to know everything. His mind was wide open to me anytime I wanted to access it. I was hurting him with my actions and he didn't deserve that.

"I was just wishing I could freeze time right now," I said, trailing my hand along his defined chest muscles. "I just want to stay in this room with you forever. Because I know when we leave anything can happen." I snorted. "Hell, the world could end tomorrow. But right now everything is perfect."

"I'll keep you safe, baby." He pulled me so I was sprawled half on top of him. "And I'll make sure that this isn't the last perfect moment we have."

His mouth captured mine and for a little while longer I could pretend that Brace would always be mine and that I never had to give him up.

"Tell me about your sister," I said hours later as we lay in the darkness.

He laughed. "Caty was the biggest pain in my ass. She was a lot younger, by almost fifty years, and I was pretty happy being an only child at that

271

point." His arms tightened around me. "I maintained that I didn't want her right up to the point she opened her massive brown eyes, wrapped her hand around my little finger and captured my heart." His voice lowered.

"She kept me on my toes. Unnaturally beautiful and the daughter of the Princeps, there used to be battles and balls to win her hand. I might have had to remind a few Walkers of their manners." I could hear the smile in his voice.

"If she's dead, a piece of me will die with her, but I'll eventually come to accept her fate." His tone changed then as he bit out the final words. "But I can't live with the thought that she's alive, suffering the way that those in the dark mountain were."

"Is there no way to track the energy of a family member?" I snuggled in to him as close as I could, offering comfort.

"There are a few things we tried, but there was nothing to be found. It's so strange because even if she was dead her energy should still be somewhere. We decide what happens to our energy, but it's as if hers is completely gone."

"What happens when you're reborn? Do you remember your last life?"

He shook his head. "No, I've been reborn once. I don't have any knowledge of my past life, except that I had one."

My head shot up. I had no idea he had lived a past life. There were so many things I needed to find out about him. And I had been counting on an eternity to discover them, but who knew now what the future would hold. I had that feeling then, in my throat where the tears were trying to claw their way from my chest and burst out of my eyes. But I refused to let them. Now was not the time for crying; it was for loving Brace with every fiber of my soul.

Hours later the rumbling of my stomach could not be ignored any longer.

"Trying to tell me something, Red?" Brace's chest shook with laughter.

"I'm starving." I groaned as I wrapped my arms around my stomach and rolled left to right on the bed. "Feed me or I'll die."

He was out of the bed faster than I could blink and I was over his shoulder.

"Never let it be said that I let my woman starve. You demand food and food you shall have." He strode from the room, both of us naked as the day of our birth.

"Uh, Brace, what about Lucy and –"

I never got to finish before my tiny blond friend, who'd clearly heard our voices, was standing before us. I lifted my head in time to see her grind to a halt, mouth open and hands dropping to her side. And as per usual Lucy she didn't avert her eyes.

"Should I be blushing right now?" Brace asked, a grin curving the corner of his mouth.

"Dude, you should be prancing around like the prize horse in a stud." Lucy lifted her brows and smirked. "Abigail did not do … all of that," she waved her hand at him, "justice."

"Lucy," I huffed. "Try to find some decorum."

She cracked up. "Abbs, your bare ass is in the air at the moment. Maybe not the time for a lecture on decorum."

She made a good point.

"Where's Colt?" I asked, really hoping he wasn't about to see me naked.

"He just left to get us all some food. That's why I was coming to find you." She grinned again. "We figured you'd need some sustenance soon. Can't live on love, you know."

I didn't completely agree with her.

"We'll meet you in the main dining area in a short while," Brace said as he turned and took us back to the bedroom.

Over his shoulder Lucy caught my eye and mouthed one word – wow. I laughed to myself.

He set me on my feet. "Sorry about that. I tend to lose all focus when I'm around you."

I stood on tiptoes and kissed him. "No girl is going to complain about that." I dropped down. "And where are my clothes?"

Brace opened an adjoining door I hadn't noticed. Stepping through, I gasped.

"Okay, now I understand why I didn't need to bring anything," I said, running my hand along the closest rack of dresses. "It's a shop. In your house." I looked at him. "Why do you have a clothes, shoes, toiletries, and homewares shop in your house?"

He laughed. "Princeps get given a lot of things. Some has been gifted recently, but most are from Que and Lasandra, my mother. Take whatever you want."

I gave him the smallest grin. "Uh, when you get dressed you should tell Lucy to have a look." This was her dream come true.

By the time Lucy and I sat down for dinner, the wild beast and vegetable dish was pretty cold. We may have spent an unnecessary amount of time in the room of unwanted gifts. If I hadn't been starving and threatening Lucy with death I'd never have gotten her out. I'd dumped my choice on the bed and hightailed it for food. After scoffing down the cold but delicious selection, my stomach finally stopped grumbling.

"Colt and I have to leave for a council meeting," Brace said as he shifted his chair back and stood. "I'd invite you, but I remember your snore-inducing love of these things."

I laughed. "Lucy and I will find something to do."

"If Red doesn't have to go then neither am I." Colton leaned back in his chair, arms crossed over his chest. "I'm not in the mood and my wolf's likely to rip the shit out of someone."

Brace kicked out the legs of his chair, landing him on the floor. "If I have to go then so do you."

"You're the damn Princeps," Colton grumbled, getting to his feet.

"And you're my second. Neither of us have a choice." Brace reached down to pull me from my chair. "Trust me, I wouldn't be leaving if I had a choice." He kissed me twice, before setting me down and leaving the room.

Colton sighed and gave Lucy and me a kiss on the cheek before slowly moving toward the door.

"Move your ass, Colt, or I'll break it." Brace's words had no visible effect on his friend's speed.

"So …" Lucy said, pushing back from the dinner table. "What ya wanna do?"

"I think we're overdue some girl talk." I moved to link arms with her. "Let's find ourselves a comfy seat."

Lucy laughed. "Oh, yeah, we have so much to discuss, like how the eff does that fit –"

I cut her off with a hand over her mouth. "If you mention Brace's naked anything I am going to hurt you."

She was pouting as I pulled my hand away. "You're no fun."

I knew where the day room was from our previous tour. It was the one with the large squishy chairs. We threw ourselves back and I swear landed onto a cloud of beauty.

"I think this is made from the hair of a Greek god," Lucy said. "Have you ever felt anything so divine?"

"So spill." I turned my head to see her. "What the heck is going on with you and Colt?"

Her features froze, and then I saw something on her face I'd never seen when she was with Samuel. Panic laced with pain.

"Oh, eff, you love him." I reached out and captured her hand. "Tell me everything."

"Well," she said slowly, "I know why he thinks he's broken, and I'm not sure there's any future for us."

"Are you mates?" I asked. "Can Earthlings and Walkers be true mates?"

She shrugged. "I thought what Samuel and I had was real, but now that Colt's in my life I know that Sammy was just a drop in the ocean of real love. Colt won't tell me if we're mates. He won't talk about it because he doesn't think it's safe for us to be together."

She laughed. "But we could be mates because I have some news. You don't have to worry about my death from old-age."

My head shot up at these words. "What do you mean?"

"I'm not from Earth," she said. "I was born on First World."

"How do you know that?"

"A vision," she said simply. "I'm half First Worlder and half pixie."

I just stared at her for an extended minute. "Did you just say pixie? Is that why you can fly?"

She laughed. "Yes, apparently that's why I'm not leggy like the rest of First World inhabitants. The legend of the pixies is actually true. They're one of First World's oldest creatures. I asked Josian about it just before we left, and he said that as far as he knows there're no pixies left." She shrugged. "But my visions tells me that they're out there, hiding for some reason."

I hugged her hard. "Thank god. I'm so glad you're not an Earthling. I need you to live forever with me. And I guess you're right: you and Colt could be true mates. We know from my parents that there's compatibility between our worlds."

"Magenta and Petal are the last of his family members." Lucy whispered the words. "And he blames himself for the death of the others."

"What happened?" I asked. "What did he show you earlier?"

"Graves," Lucy murmured, her eyes staring off into space. "There were so many, spanning as far as I could see."

"Aren't they Walkers?" I was confused. "How could they all be dead?"

Lucy shook out her blond curls. "It's complex but something to do with the wolf in their family tree. Apparently his father's wolf went crazy and killed the rest. Colt said his wolf can kill Walkers."

"How is that Colt's fault?"

"I was off being an arrogant dick on another world," Colton's voice sounded from behind us, "when I should have been here protecting my family and stopping my father."

"You know that's stupid, right?" Lucy stood, hands on her hips as she faced him. "You are not responsible for someone else's actions. You couldn't have known what was happening. And you at least had Magenta with you."

Brace stepped in behind him. "Sorry, baby, we just forgot a few things. We have to go again." He laid a hand on Colton's shoulder. "And I was on First World when this happened. Que stepped in and saved Petal, but it was too late for everyone else."

"He saved Petal because she was a child," I guessed.

Colt laughed; it was strangled and rasping. "He would never admit that. He just said he didn't arrive in time to save any but her. But really Que cared for no one but himself, so probably he couldn't be bothered to save the rest."

"And I still don't understand how this misplaced guilt you carry means we can never be together?" Lucy challenged him again.

Colton strode across to her, getting right into her face. He was almost bent in half to meet her gaze.

"My father was a good man. The wolf tore through that, and then with no thought for those that the Walker loved, it killed everyone. I can never trust my wolf."

Lucy snorted. "You have loved ones already, dumbass. Magenta, Petal, Brace. There's no difference. And anyone could go nuts and start offing people. Shit, it could be me who snaps next. I do have an awful lot of voices in my head. I know the danger, I accept it, and it's my choice to make."

"No." Fear darkened his features. "I will never risk you." He strode from the room.

"Come on, Brace," he yelled as the front door slammed.

"I'll talk to him," Brace promised as he touched my face once and left.

Lucy stared out at the empty doorway for a moment. She might have wiped away a tear, but by the time she faced me her expression was calm.

"It's for the best," she said before I could open my mouth. "You have to break the melding bond, and it would be better if I didn't have ties to Colt. You'll need the distance."

I huffed. Her drama had allowed me to temporarily forget about my future, and then back it came to kick me in the butt.

"Two days," I said to Lucy. "We have two days with the boys that are free from our problems. Let's take this time for all the moments we'll have without them."

She stood straighter and nodded once. "Yes. I vote for two days where we don't mention any of our problems."

"They don't even exist."

"Hey, Abbs, did I tell you I can fly?"

I laughed. "I can forget some things, but that is permanently burned into my memory."

When Brace and Colton returned they had Petal with them. She was a ball of energy running around the room, dancing to music only she could hear and jumping all over her Bwacie and Cowt. I couldn't remember laughing so much in my life; she was a true delight. So much innocence, untouched by her family tragedy. And then when her eyelids grew heavy she crawled into my lap. My heart almost burst as she snuggled her head into me and fell asleep.

As I stroked her hair I looked up to catch Brace's eye. He smiled gently, his entire face softening. He took the seat next to me and the three of us cuddled together for a while.

"Who does she live with," I asked Colton softly, "when you and Magenta aren't here?"

He shifted from where he was sprawled on the floor. "Petal lives with her father. He was never mated to my sister. He was her friend, so when she wanted a child he volunteered."

I'd assumed he'd also died in Colton's father's attack, so it was nice to know Petal still had her dad.

"He's a good man. Which lets me rest easy when I'm not here for Pet."

After a while I started to drift off, the warmth and sweet smell of Petal lulling me right to sleep.

I tightened my arms as I felt her weight shift.

"Let Colt put her to bed, love." Brace's voice calmed me.

I opened my eyes long enough to see Colton take Petal into the first bedroom. He was back in no time as he gathered Lucy into his arms.

"I'll watch over them tonight," he said. "You two get some rest."

Brace hauled me into his arms.

"I can walk," I mumbled sleepily.

Of course, as I said that, I was burrowing in as close to him as I could.

He laughed. "I got you, Red, go to sleep."

"Whatever you say."

It's a rare gift to feel so safe that you could sleep soundly.

Brace woke me early the next morning. Normally I'd have had to punch him for that, but his delicate kisses were so delicious that there was nothing to complain about.

"Get dressed," he whispered to me. "There's something I want to show you."

I didn't hesitate. Brace could lead me through the gates of hell and I'd be the one throwing shoes and sunscreen in my bag. I didn't care where he took me. I shimmied into a pair of jeans, then threw on a white long-sleeved ribbed tank, my trusty boots and a jacket. It took me less than a minute to braid my hair.

Once I was finished I spun around only to find a naked Brace sprawled on the bed, his dark eyes locked on me.

My hands flew to my hips. "What are you doing?"

The slightest grin crossed his lips as he pulled himself to stand. I lost my train of thought for a moment as I watched him. All grace and muscles. It took him no time to dress.

"I couldn't miss the show," he murmured as he gathered me into his arms.

I snorted. "I hope that wasn't the reason you woke me at the ass-crack of morning."

His chest shook with laughter. "You have such a way with words, Red. And no, you have to see the sunrise on Abernath."

It was dark and cold outside. The only lights to break the surroundings were those from a few stray windows. Electricity worked here in the same manner as on First World; energy absorbed from the sun was stored in the buildings and used for power. Walkers could use their own energy, but this was easier.

We hiked for a short distance to one of the edges of town and then out into the forest. As we moved on a path through the trees, I noticed a steady incline. By the time we cleared the forest and made it to the peak of the hill a huge ball of light was starting to crest the horizon.

"Oh, my god." I breathed in the early morning air, so crisp and tart. "I can see the whole city."

I was able to really observe Abernath: the main town and then so much of the natural habitat around it. The sun continued to rise. It was so close I felt as if I could reach out and touch its burning surface.

"Turn around," Brace said at my back.

I spun slowly and more gasps fell from my mouth. There were four suns. I'd thought that the sky was a strong yellow with one sun, but in reality four globes filled the sky and produced the yellow color.

"I'd hazard a guess that they're a mix between an Earth sun and moon. Not very hot, but providing life-giving energy," Brace said.

I turned my face from the wonder of watching the four suns rise right before me to stare at Brace.

"We're so close to them. And damn they move fast."

The orbs were already halfway into the sky.

Brace didn't remove his eyes from where they were locked on my face.

"Is there something you want to tell me, Abigail?"

Oh, shit. Clearly I hadn't been as good at hiding my plans as I thought. Lucy was going to kill me. The question was how much did he know?

"What do you mean?" I was proud that my voice did not waver.

He took a step closer to me. "I get the distinct feeling you're about to do something stupid."

Huh? Ass.

"Something which you think is noble and brave and that you have to do alone. But in reality it will be stupid. Because we're stronger together, as a pair, and I know when you don't confide in me it's because you're either protecting me, or worried about how I'll react." He gripped my biceps gently. "If it involves us, then I think I need to know."

I sucked in a breath. Lucy was wrong; I had to tell him. It wasn't really my place to make this decision for Brace. For us. I was just opening my mouth to spill everything, when a shout distracted us.

"There you are!" Lucy and Colton scrambled up the last of the hill. "How amazing is this?" Lucy continued to chat in a frantic and friendly tone, but I could see the panic in her blue eyes.

Once she reached me she took my hand, pulling me a little from Brace. My eyes narrowed; she never did things like that. What was going on with her?

"Mind if I borrow Abbs? Need a quick girl chat." She grinned at the boys and tugged on my arm until I followed her.

Her smile never wavered as she leaned in close. "Can they still hear me?"

I could barely hear her mutter. I shook my head.

"Don't tell Brace," was her next statement. "If you tell him we all die."

"Did you have another vision?" My lip trembled. I bit down hard to stop it.

She nodded. "Yes, and it was worse than last time."

So that's why she'd dragged Colton up here.

I could feel his stare and I couldn't stop my head from rising to meet the worried gaze of my mate. I forced my face into lines of happiness. I think there was even a smile. Our fate was set now; I had no choice.

Chapter 15

We were back on First World. The last few days on Abernath had been like a dream. A perfect romantic fantasy, which showed me the exact life I could have had with Brace if the Seventine weren't threatening to destroy everything I cared about.

Bastards.

The four of us were sitting on the front grassed area at the Angelisian house, waiting for everyone to join us. The street fair would start in a few hours. Lallielle had been off frantically organizing when I got back. While we waited I couldn't stop thinking about something which had begun to niggle away at me the previous night.

"What do you think Olden meant when she said we don't even know why they've chosen this time to start releasing the Seventine?" I spoke out loud.

Brace, Colton and Lucy turned toward me.

"Is there some significance that we missed? I always thought it had something to do with us half-Walkers, but maybe it's something else."

Brace straightened. "You're right. We've been so focused on stopping their release that no one has really questioned why, in the thousands of years of imprisonment, it's now that they're free."

"There must be something significant about this time," I said.

Another thought was bothering me. I felt as if I'd been told the answer to this second question but couldn't remember it. Then it hit me. A handsome face flashed across my mind. Jedi, the dark-skinned Princeps of Gai, had told me to find him when I questioned why. Was this what he had meant?

I was distracted then as the black clouds which had been threatening all day exploded in torrents of rain. With a shriek I followed everyone up under the shelter of the front stoop. I moved so quickly that I was there without even having one drop land on me. The gravity on First World was so weak compared to Abernath that I almost felt as if I could float.

"Oh, my god." Fury dashed out the front door. "I've been waiting forever to see rain."

She was followed by Dune, who swept her off her feet and spun the pair in circles.

Ria paused next to me. "Wow. We have nothing but a damp mist on Regali. This is incredible." And then she too was out running.

From the ocean rose Talina and Ladre. The pair held hands as they left the waves and frolicked in the streaming rain. I looked at Lucy, who gave me a wicked grin, and without any more wasted time we sprinted out to join our friends. We had so much fun. The grass turned into a muddy mess and I found myself slipping and falling onto my face more than once. By the time an amused Josian and Lallielle appeared we were all covered head to toe in mud.

"Come on." Josian waved us in with a grin. "As fun as that looks, it's time to get dressed."

"Will the rain ruin the fair?" I asked Lallielle.

She smiled. "It will just be a short rain burst. Everything will go ahead as planned."

When we were all clean and dressed, we stepped outside to find a clear afternoon sky. Lallielle was right. I had on a bright yellow dress; even with the rain it wasn't cold enough to need more than a cardigan.

"Weird to see you in a dress. You look beautiful," Lucy said.

"Thanks. You too." I gave her a smile.

She wore all white, which made her look far more angelic than I knew she was.

As a group we strolled along the paved streets of Angelisian. I could hear the music ahead of us, but so far couldn't see the fair or street parade set up.

"It's a bit smaller than usual," Lallielle explained as we moved closer. "But considering it came together in only a couple of days, I'm still happy with the final results."

Josian laughed. "I have no doubt it's above and beyond what anyone else could have done."

And, knowing Lallielle, Josian was totally correct.

There were a few people walking around us, some further in front and others behind. The people of Angelisian dressed in old-fashioned clothing, using stunning colors and material, but they were much more demure than anything we wore on Earth. On the women, dresses were no shorter than calf-length. Sleeves appeared to be a must. The men wore tailored pants and robe-style shirts.

"First Worlders are a little bit classier than the gangers of Earth," Lucy said as she noticed where my attention was.

I snorted. "Oh, yeah, just a little. Must be the lack of facial tattoos."

Not to mention absolutely everything else.

A group of six rounded the corner in front of us, and as we followed their path into the town center the noise intensified around us. My smile grew as I took in the colorful scene. There were so many people, the most I had ever seen in Angelisian. They mingled amongst dozens of brightly patterned cloth tented stalls, and I could see each held a variety of foods, wares and … well, I wasn't exactly sure what some of them were.

"I am so freaking hungry," Lucy said as she pumped her little arms to march quicker into the square. "How does it work with paying for things?"

Lallielle laughed. "There's no barter or exchange for anything here. This is a celebration, and all are welcome to sample the goods provided by different families. But you better get in quick before the best stuff disappears."

We walked through the main thoroughfare and Lallielle explained what each of the food tents had, who the families were and which dishes she recommended. Most of our group disappeared then, off to explore and eat. Brace and I stayed with my parents. I was interested in hearing the history of the families as we passed them.

Then we came to a small pavilion and I let out a loud breath as I realized what I was seeing.

Paintings, of many differing shapes and sizes, and I recognized the bold use of color and pattern.

"Mom," I exclaimed. "Are these all yours?"

Lallielle moved into the center of the exhibition. "Yes, I've been painting again. Your return triggered my creative muse."

"And we are grateful." A voice spoke from behind us. "I have been waiting a long time for one of Lalli's original pieces."

The speaker was a tall, broad woman, with shoulder-length brown hair, olive skin and brown eyes.

"Cherry." Lallielle moved forward to embrace her. "Aribella ... Brace, this is one of our neighbors."

Introductions were made all round. The woman was friendly with a practical personality. Eventually she left clutching a mid-size piece of art, which was predominantly in the cool tones of blue and purple.

I took a step back as Lucas emerged through the crowds now gathered around Lallielle's display. He was followed closely by the weathered features of Quarn. The Emperor was thankfully minus the massive crown and jeweled cloak, but still wore an official-looking headpiece and long black robes.

Ignoring him for the moment, I threw myself into my guardian's arms for a proper hug. I couldn't believe I'd come so close to losing him.

"I hear we owe you thanks for the return of many missing First Worlders," Lucas said as I pulled back and acknowledged the Emperor. "You're powerful, Abby. You would be a huge asset to the ruling body."

"I'm trying to save an entire star-system." My tone was flat. I'd repeated this far too many times to him. "I don't have time or interest in ruling as Empress."

As usual my words did nothing to deter him. He just continued. "There's something different about you." He stepped closer, looking confused. "What's changed?"

"She's accepted her part as my mate and Princeps of Abernath." Brace spoke up, shifting me closer to him. "You sense the new energy inside her."

Finally a change crossed Lucas' icy features. He looked unhappy. "You can't keep dividing your loyalties. One day you have to make a choice."

"My choice was made for me long before I ever met you. Brace is my mate," I replied.

But I knew that soon the bond would be broken. I wondered what that spelled for my argument.

"Emperor, you are needed at the Hawthorne display." A bland voice sounded from behind Lucas.

I hadn't even noticed the stiff man standing there. He seemed to be an advisor of sorts, but he blended in so well with the scenery he was almost unnoticeable.

"Right." Lucas nodded his blond head. "You should check this out, Abby. This family don't display their gifts very often, and it's quite the sight to behold."

He left as quickly as he had come. The creeper followed closely behind.

I looked at Quarn. "The Hawthornes?" I questioned.

He laughed. "They're mesmerizers."

We started to move, pushing through the masses of people that were suddenly everywhere. I thought back to my first conversation with Brace about the gifts of First World. He had said something about not trusting mesmerizers. I was really interested to see what they did.

Their tent was large, in a dark blue color. There were four of them standing there: two men and two women.

"The blond woman and red-haired man are the parents." Brace leaned down to speak in my ear. "The children are said to be much more powerful."

The children, who weirdly looked the same age as their parents, were both brown-haired and slender. They looked like twins.

"Greetings, fellow Angelisians and guests. And, importantly, Emperor Lucas."

As the red-haired man started to speak I noticed that Lucas was across from us on the other side of the tent space.

"Thank you for honoring us. We will now display our skills."

The act started out simple enough. They called for volunteers from the audience and proceeded to make each of them perform strange, uncomfortable and downright impossible tasks. I resisted the urge to put my hand up. I was pretty sure their skills wouldn't work on me, but in the end I let them have their moment of power.

"And now for our grand finale." It was the blond mother who spoke this time.

The group of four stepped forward and reached out to grasp each other's hands. They closed their eyes. I waited for a few moments, wondering what was happening, and then it burst from them.

It was like a scene from a movie, or a backdrop to a theatre production. And it felt as if we were standing right in the middle of it. I could still see the Angelisian fair right behind the cloak of a desert island that surrounded us.

"I'm not sure about you, but the First Worlders cannot see anything but the island," Quarn muttered. "I've heard it doesn't work so well on Walkers."

I shook my head. "I can see the island, but it's fuzzy, like a veil hovering over the real scene."

It was a powerful gift. Everyone in the vicinity was truly mesmerized by what they saw. None even shifted during the entire time until the Hawthornes finally released their hands and the power abated.

Most of the crowd clapped their efforts before moving on to other areas.

I reached out and threaded my fingers through Brace's. We started to move with the dispersing crowd, passing many of the other family display tents. Quarn stayed with us as our very knowledgeable tour guide.

"The Swarne family is blessed with animal affinity." He pointed toward a low-slung, yellow tent where half a dozen men crouched around small penned-off areas.

As we stepped closer, I was astonished by the very unusual animals that were scattered around. They ranged from a scaled creature that looked like a cross between a monitor and small dragon, a dog, a big cat that reminded me of a mane-less lion, an aquatic animal in a tank, and a few bird species. None of these were animals found on Earth, so I could only guess at their abilities.

We watched for a few minutes. The Swarne men had the animals performing tricks, singing in their animal sounds, and interacting with each other. It was a very interesting gift and I loved to see the family's obvious love for their animals. We moved again and the next booth we passed was filled with plants, to the point where I couldn't even see any people in there.

"Nature spirits," Quarn said. "Watch closely.

I concentrated more, trying my best to really see into the tent. The plants were dense. I could feel warm and damp heat from the area, and everything inside was moving, shifting around. I wasn't surprised, as we stepped a little closer, to find Ria standing before it.

"This is beautiful. Tell me of these vines." She was talking to … a plant it looked like.

But at that moment I finally saw them. First World people were inside the mass of greenery, almost like living plants themselves. They were green and blended into their environment perfectly. Shaking my head at their incredible camouflage skills, we left Ria chatting away to the green people and continued on.

"They have developed the ability to change their skin tone and reflect their environment," Quarn said.

"Walkers are dominant in this star-system," Brace said as he looked around. "But we can't discount the abundance of gifts here also. Some of these families are very old and very powerful."

By this time I was starving so we quickly bypassed the family who were emoters. I was amazed to see how easily they manipulated emotions around them. In one corner people were laughing deliriously, the other they were crying, tears running silently down their cheeks. I was already emotionally out of whack, so I didn't need any help from them that day.

Brace led me to the stall with the fruit salad cups and large trays of rice and meat dishes. This had been my choice when Lallielle had pointed out the food earlier. He must have picked up my thought.

My heart stuttered a little then.

I'd been steadfastly ignoring the fact I had to break the bond after this. I really just wanted to enjoy whatever time I had with him. But every little reminder of how amazing he was, and how perfectly we fit together, was like being stabbed in the heart.

If the Seventine had been there right then, I'd have tried walking up to them and ripping their damn heads off. It just wasn't fair, but at the end of the day things in life rarely are. It's not like the bad people are the ones who suffer, and the good ones get their just rewards. In my experience it was generally the opposite way. And if karma was real, then it was not holding up its end of the bargain.

Quarn paused at the food stall.

"I need to make sure that the Emperor is fine and that no one attempts to assassinate him tonight." His eyes flicked to me when he said that.

I shrugged. "I'm not promising anything, but right now food is my priority, so Lucas is safe."

With a shake of his head Quarn left us there.

After grabbing two big orders of food, Brace and I sat at the top of the hill, which gave us a great view down into the town center. I started shoveling in spoonfuls, or, as they called them here: shavel fulls, of the delicious and aromatic food. My attention wavered for a moment as a strange sight to my left caught my eye.

"What the hell?" I muttered, shifting my head to the side to see clearer. "Are they naked?"

Brace laughed. "Moonlighters. They're the Earth equivalent of a hippy. The moonlights give them energy. They roam around at night, naked under their source of life."

They were literally frolicking. With a shake of my head, I averted my eyes.

"Sometimes, in moments like this," Brace had finished his food and was leaning back on his arms, "I forget that someone is trying to destroy the worlds."

"Who do you think the big bad guys are?" I'd been trying to figure it out ever since Olden and the room of horrors, but I had no idea who trumped the Walkers in power.

"I really did think this originated with Que," Brace said. "I mean, there are other creatures, like you saw with the tree-spirits on Regali. Most of the worlds have their spirits and gods, but nothing really tops Walkers."

I leaned forward to rest my arms on my knees. "I suppose that doesn't mean something else hasn't figured out how to manipulate the system and still release the Seventine, even if they aren't the most powerful."

Brace nodded. "Yeah, that's kind of where I'm leaning right now. Or there's another Walker who somehow is bigger and badder than Que and has been hidden forever."

I kept getting the strange feeling that our bad guy was closer to home than we could ever have imagined.

"Hey, Abbs," Lucy shouted as she found our lofty spot.

She was followed by the rest of the group. Fury and Dune had some type of rolled salad sandwich. Talina and Ladre were both wearing large brimmed hats on their luscious hair, despite the fact it was night now. Colton strolled up. He had one hand tightly entwined with Lucy's.

He noticed me looking. "She's tiny," he finally said. "I kept losing her in the crowd; this just seemed easiest."

Lucy snorted. "Yeah, I was afraid he wanted to hook me up to one of those backpacks with the leads. You know, the ones they used on Earth for rambunctious toddlers."

Colton leaned in really close to her face and I could see her freeze in his presence. "I have never once thought of you as a child, Lucy, not for a damn second."

"Those two need to just hook up and get over this," Fury said. "This whole build-up, sexual-tension thing is even killing me, and I'm getting plenty."

I couldn't help myself: I burst into laughter. Fury was growing on me. Her snarkiness was so refreshing.

Lucy meanwhile was staring expectantly at Colton. "As much as I love to annoy Fury, she's got a point.

Colton stared at her. She stood there in her lace dress, all white and angel-like in the moonlight, and then he growled, low in his throat.

"Dammit," he said as he reached down and threw her over his shoulder. "I can't fight against her any longer. She's some type of witch and I'm hooked."

"Don't wait up," Lucy all but shrieked.

They were just turning to leave when Samuel stepped out of the shadows to stand before them.

Oh, eff. This was not good.

Samuel and Francesca had decided at the last minute not to attend the fair. They were still recovering from their months of imprisonment. So what the hell was he doing here now, ruining Lucy's moment?

"Sammy." Lucy wiggled until Colton set her down before him. "What are you doing here?"

"We need to talk, Luce. Before you make any choices, I need you to know my side of the story."

Colton stepped in front of Lucy then. His eyes had shifted color and his words came out in low growls.

"She's mine." His presence went from jovial to menacing in a heartbeat. "You didn't treasure her, and now I claim her as my mate."

Lucy's face softened as she threaded her fingers through Colton's, pulling him back to her side. He visibly calmed under her touch.

"I don't need to hear your words, Sammy," Lucy said, without taking her eyes from Colton. "I already forgive you, but my life is with Colt. I have no doubts what a true bond is now."

Samuel features, so much like Lallielle's, hardened and he didn't back down from the threatening aura Colton was throwing his way.

"It's not over. I'll wait for you, Lucy. I told you once I was the guy for you and that's still true. This animal is nothing more than a passing fancy."

Brace got to Colton before he reached Samuel. "Calm, old friend." He spoke in a low soothing voice. "Walk away now, Sammy. Colt will rip your god-damned head off."

Samuel hesitated, throwing one last look at Lucy before gritting his teeth and storming off.

It took Lucy and Brace a few minutes to bring Colton back. He was half-shifting into a wolf as we watched. He never took his eyes off Lucy the entire time.

"I told you my wolf is unstable," he finally said when his eyes were back to their light blue.

Brace was the one doing the growling now. "You never hurt anyone, Colt. If anything you reacted as any mate would. Less than me."

"Word," I said to that.

Brace shook his head at me.

"She's my mate," Colton said as he hauled Lucy into his arms. "And I'm afraid I'll kill anyone who takes her from me."

He got serious then as he stared down at her. "But if you choose to walk away, I will let you."

She laughed. "If Abbs and Brace's lovefest has taught me anything, it's that you can't fight fate or a true mate. You're not getting rid of me that easily."

He kissed her then, and it was everything a first kiss should be. The moment almost stood still for them and I knew I wasn't the only one holding my breath.

When they finally pulled apart, Colton snuggled her under his arm. She met my gaze and I saw so much happiness there, but also a bit of pain. She mouthed 'sorry' to me.

I shook my head. I knew she felt as if she'd made things a lot worse. Her tie to Colton would be an obstacle to breaking my melding bond, but life could be short for us all and we needed to take happiness wherever we could find it.

Chapter 16

I stood on the sand, ocean water washing over my toes. I was avoiding the fact that I had to pull myself together and focus on the two tasks that were next on my list. I needed to speak with Jedi, because I was definitely questioning why now. And I needed to break the melding bond with Brace. Both were urgent and both could spell the difference in our battle against the Seventine.

"Baby?" Brace strode across the sand toward me.

Upon returning from the fair we had all gathered on the front lawn for a nightcap. I'd only just strolled down to the water, needing a few minutes.

"I need to head back to Abernath for a couple of days. Do you want to come with me?"

More than anything in this or the seven worlds.

I gave him a half-smile. "I'd love to, but I have to get back to my mission. Josian and I need to discuss some strategies for the next world, and the four of us girls have to practice with our powers. We don't even know what Ria can really do yet."

He nodded. "Keep me updated on where you're at, and don't go to Nephilius without me."

I laughed and saluted him. "Yes, sir."

He kissed me on the lips. "Smartass." His words were soft, and with one last gentle touch he left me on the beach.

Last kiss. I reached up and touched my fingertips to my tingling lips. Our last kiss.

I didn't have time to fall apart now so I traced into my bedroom to change my clothes to jeans and a shirt. Dresses were not ideal for most of my adventures.

Striding downstairs, I found Josian. He was standing with Lallielle, just holding her. His eyes met mine over my mother's shoulder, and he must have seen the resignation there.

It was time.

He nodded once and then flicked his head toward the door. He wanted me to wait out there for him.

I stayed in the shadows, not wanting to draw the attention of my friends. This needed to stay a secret for many reasons.

"What are you doing, Abigail?" a voice drawled.

I jumped about a foot in the air.

"Goddamn sneaky soothsayers," I said, one hand on my chest as I stared at Lucy. "How did you know I was here?"

"Don't think for one second that you're doing this without me," she said, her hands on her hips. "You'll need someone to lean on. Someone to cry with. I'm your girl."

"I would never have left without you. We've been in this together since the beginning." I reached out and captured her hand. "Where's Colt?" I was surprised he'd let her out of his sight.

"I convinced him that he needed to watch Brace's back for a while. You know, newly crowned Princeps and all. I said we'd come to Abernath later." Her eyes fell. "I know now why you've objected so strongly to keeping this from Brace. Even a small lie has my heart aching and my mind rebelling the concept."

I sighed as tears pricked my eyes. "Yes, just wait until you perform the mating ceremony and Colton is in your mind. When you lie to him it'll feel as if you're lying to yourself. It's wrong on so many levels."

"Colt wants to do it straight away," she said in a low voice. "I feel I can't do that to you, Abbs, but I'm not sure how to hold him off."

I forced a smile. "Your happiness is my happiness. Don't delay anything for me."

Lucy was my sister and always had been. Obviously our ties to First World had drawn us together all of those years ago. For all I knew she'd been put in the same compound as me for a reason.

She grimaced. "The way things are going for us, I won't have to delay. This damn mission will delay for us."

On the grassed area Fury was now running around, covered in her flames. I shook my head as Talina followed suit, sending jets of water in her direction. The flames sizzled but re-flared after each geyser.

"At least some are enjoying the night," Josian said, becoming the second person to almost give me a heart attack that night. "Are you sure you want to do this, baby girl?"

"I'd rather have my finger nails pulled out one by one than break the melding bond." I grimaced. "But the world needs to be saved, yada yada."

I wasn't really that uncaring about the worlds, but right then their neediness didn't make me happy. Take, take, take is all they did. It was starting to feel like a one-sided relationship. Of the abusive kind.

"Okay, then let's go speak to someone who may be able to help you." Josian opened a doorway and, with Lucy between us, we stepped in.

As we moved through I recognized the stone room at the end. Josian's planet.

He had opened it into the garden area and straight away I knew where he was taking me. The lalunas. And, judging by Lucy's wide eyes, she'd also realized.

"Now, it's better if I deal with them. They can be a little strange. Their minds are ancient and don't always think the same way as you and I," he warned as we moved across the rocks and around to the hidden alcove.

I had to hide my smile. I wasn't sure Josian thought like us either.

As we stood before the little fairy world, they emerged, one by one, their ethereal, almost wispy bodies draped in sheer silk. The female that had spoken to us before stepped forward and onto Josian's hand.

"We missed you," she said, cuddling into his palm. "You've been gone forever."

He smiled gently at the crazy little fairy. One look at her face left me with no doubt that she was bonkers.

"Ahh, Tenni, I visit as often as I can. Do you need anything?"

She shook her head, wings fluttering. "No, we have all of the worlds here."

That was a weird thing to say.

"I need you to do something for me," Josian said, carefully picking over his words. "Can you break a melding bond?"

Her tinkling laughter echoed around the cavernous garden area. "You know that there is very little we can't do." She rose off his hand. "It is for you?" She addressed the last words to me.

I nodded, not moving closer.

"Because you are our bonded one's beloved daughter. We will help you."

Josian placed her back down in the garden where a hundred faces watched us.

"Do you understand what you are asking, though?"

I swallowed. This didn't sound good.

"There is no way to truly break something as ancient as a melding bond. It is the same as the birth of yin and yang. Two sides of the same coin. I can sever the cord, but there will be remnants of the connection."

"Will my power no longer be merged with his?"

"Your power will be your own, but the heart is another matter."

I nodded. This was my best chance.

"What will the side-effects be?" Lucy said, ignoring Josian's initial request to let him do the speaking.

"When we sever the cord we will remove the memories of Aribella and Brace from all except you three. You must make sure that there is no chance to reform the melding bond."

"Brace won't remember me?" Tears pricked at my eyes.

All of our perfect memories just stolen from him. I thought I'd have the chance to explain after it was done, when he could no longer stop me. Explain why I had to do this, but that couldn't happen now.

"So how do we stop them reforming the bond?" Lucy spoke again.

"They must never touch under the light of our precious moonstale," she trilled. "And be warned, if you decide to reform the melding bond it may never be as it is now. What is broken does not always be fixed."

Crazy-ass fairy.

Josian met my gaze. I smiled, albeit in a wavering manner.

"No choice, remember."

He turned to his lalunas. "Let's do this."

She nodded, fluttering closer. The rest of the lalunas gathered around her. "Do you agree to the terms? You will owe us a future favor?"

Josian cleared his throat. "I agree to take this debt."

She shook her head. "No, it must be Aribella, for this is her debt to incur."

I waved my hands at them. "Yes, yes, that's fine. Let's get this done before I change my mind." I clenched my hands into fists at my side.

"Excellent." Tenni's little eyes glittered, reminding me of Brace's warning never to trust them.

I could feel their buildup of power. The cavern started to shake as the lalunas joined hands.

I opened my bond for the last time.

Red?

Brace sounded confused. I hadn't opened the bond fully for a long time.

I love you and I will find a way to be with you again, in this life or the next.

I could feel his horror as he sifted through my thoughts. I knew it was okay because very soon he would have no memories of us.

I wanted to tell you, every day, but Lucy said everyone would die. I couldn't risk it.

His horror flooded my mind. *Stop them, Abigail. They can't be trusted and you can't break our bond.*

It's too late. The fate of millions of lives don't trump our love.

He exploded with a string of curses. *Nothing trumps our love. Why did you not trust me with this? We could have figured something out.*

Energy was shooting off in visible ricochets from the laluna and I knew our time was up.

Love you for every eternity. I said my farewell, my heart screaming, tears streaming down my cheeks.

I will come for you, Red. I will not give up without a fight. You are everything.

His voice broke.

Red ...

A roar was the last thing I heard as the energy of the lalunas struck me hard. I fell to my knees and in that moment my entire world unraveled.

Chapter 17

I was close to comatose for days. Josian and Lucy kept me on his world, secluded from everyone, and since no one remembered Brace and my melding, they had to make up something about extra training to explain my absence. Apparently Josian had to be very convincing to stop Lallielle from coming to find me. So while Lucy never left my side, Josian went back and forward between the worlds. In this time he continued to train the half-Walker females.

During those few days I'd been present in my head, but it took me awhile to piece myself back together. For some reason after Lucy's vision I expected to feel stronger in my power without Brace, once I stopped sharing with him, but to be honest I'd never felt weaker. It had to be the pain in my heart and soul that was draining my strength.

"Are you ever going to say anything, Abbs?" Lucy was holding my hand.

I'd properly awoken that morning, managed to eat some food but hadn't spoken yet. I just didn't have anything to say. Well, that wasn't completely true.

"Did Dad speak with Brace?" My voice was hoarse.

Lucy gripped my hand tighter. "Yes, he went to congratulate him as the new Princeps of Abernath."

"Did he remember?" I asked.

She shook her head. "Jos said it was weird. He remembered you and he knew everything about our mission. But it was as if the romantic moments between you and him had been removed." She cleared her throat. "Apparently he did seem confused on occasion, but that's to be expected."

"What about Colt? Does he remember you?" I wasn't sure to what extent the memories had been taken.

"Oh, yeah, he remembers." She snorted. "He hasn't been very understanding about where I am and why he can't know what happened to you."

Her sympathetic gaze met mine. "And you might have another problem."

I pulled myself up to sit. I was starting to get used to the roaring pain that was char-grilling me from the inside out. And nothing was changing soon so I might as well pull myself together.

"Hit me with it." It could be added to my list of problems a mile long.

"Lucas is demanding you return and take your place as Empress."

I shook my head. "Uh, what? Haven't I made my position on that clear to him?"

"Yes, but he's forgotten much of that, Abbs. All the memories of your bond to Brace have been removed. So Lucas doesn't know of any reason why you're not the chosen Empress, and apparently it's time to take your throne."

"Holy freaking eff."

"Word," Lucy said. "Josian has started working on him, explaining that your mission comes first. He may have bought you a little time." She shrugged. "But I've never seen Lucas so determined."

"Should have asked the lalunas to remove Lucas' memories too," I joked as I stood up.

Lucy threw me a clean set of clothes, which had been folded on the end of the bed. "Speaking of crazy little fairies," she said, "your stone has been next to you since the bond was broken."

I'd already known it was there. Its warmth and strength had been one of the things which helped me open my eyes. Picking it up, I cradled it gently in my hands.

"Thank you," I whispered as I kissed it.

It must have sensed that I was okay right then and it disappeared.

I felt Josian's power enter the cavern.

"Lucy." He strode into the room. "How's our girl doin …?"

He trailed off as he noticed me standing there. "Baby girl." His shout echoed around.

He scooped me up into his arms.

In the last ten minutes I felt as if I'd become an expert at holding the pain inside. I could smile now despite the complete void of hope and joy inside.

"I need to speak with Jedi," I said, wasting no time on other pleasantries.

If I didn't stay busy I would go nuts.

Josian regarded me carefully. "Are you sure you don't need a few more days to deal with these emotions?"

I shook my head. "No, less time to think is what I need. And the sooner I can save these worlds, the sooner I can see if there's any way to repair my relationship with Brace."

"You're strong, and I'm very proud of you. Eighteen years of life is so short to be so brave and smart." He hugged me again.

In that moment I didn't feel strong, I was like brittle glass set to shatter with a hard tap. But as long as I knew what I had to do next and took one step after another, I'd make it through the day.

"The Princeps are meeting at our place tomorrow," Josian said. "I never expected you would be awake, otherwise I would have suggested a different location. But that's going to be a good opportunity to speak with Jedi."

"But Brace will be there." Lucy's voice was tinged with horror. "Don't you think that's going to be a bit difficult?"

"Brace declined the invitation. He said he can't get away from Abernath at the moment. There's too much with becoming a new Princeps," Josian said. "I encouraged that and said I'll let him know anything that's discussed."

I straightened. "That's fine, and even if he was there, I can't avoid him forever. It'll be like ripping off a bandage: better to get it over with."

Lucy snorted. "More like ripping off a limb, but whatever you think."

Yep, she was right, but I had no problem lying to myself.

She studied me for a few moments.

"You want to see him, don't you?" Her jaw dropped. "Why?"

I sighed. She couldn't let me live a lie for five seconds.

"I need to see that he doesn't remember me. I have to make sure it worked."

"And what if it's so painful you relapse into the comatose state?" Lucy demanded. "I don't want to see you like that again."

"I won't." I was sure of that. "That was simply my mind and body adjusting to the loss of my bond." The loss of Brace in my soul.

His presence had been so warm, strong, I had never felt alone. But now the very essence of my being was rattling around an empty room alone. All alone.

"I'm so sorry that you have to go through this, sacrifice your love." Lucy's soft heart got the better of her and her eyes filled with tears.

And I knew, after Colton and the town fair, that she really understood now.

"I kind of think it was something I deserved. I should never have freed the third Seventine, whether I was manipulated or not. Now I need to earn back my love."

I straightened, pushing back my curls, determination flooding me.

"Brace and I will be together. I will fight forever for him, so for now I'll stay strong and try for some patience."

"Well, patience is not your strongest asset, but I know you can do it." Lucy wrapped me in a hug.

"I'll be glad to stop lying to your mother about your mission to find inner peace," Josian grumbled.

I grinned at him. "Did you tell her I was meditating?"

"Don't laugh; it's been very difficult. I never lie to her and she's so smart." He ran a hand through his blood-red hair. "She keeps asking me about a lotus or something, and I have no idea what to say."

Lucy and I fell into each other, laughter erupting from us. The kind of good, cleansing, chest-rattling laughter.

"Come on, comedians, let's go home." Josian opened a doorway and dragged us both through.

"Abby!" Talina was the first to run at me. "I've missed you; I'm so glad you're back." She wrapped me in her arms, her emerald hair surrounding us like a cloud.

"How is Ladre doing?" I pulled back.

She both blushed and preened. "He's amazing. Still a little scarred but much more stable than I'd be. And the best part is being away from the prejudices of Spurn and having time to actually talk." Her already pink face deepened to a rosy color. "Well, I'm finding we have a lot in common."

"I'm so happy for you." And I was.

No one deserved happiness more than gentle Talina. I just hoped Ladre loved her the way she deserved. I'd reserve judgment until I saw them together.

"Aribella." My mother's scolding tone washed over me. "Don't run off without telling me." She pulled me into a hug. "One day when you have your own children you'll understand."

I felt a little confused. No one was usually this over-protective toward me. I disappeared all the time. Granted, I usually said where I was going, but this was over-kill. Josian must have noticed my confusion.

It's because they no longer know about Brace.

I jumped as his voice sounded in my head. I hadn't dropped my barriers.

How are you in my head?

Your barriers were weak and I just pushed past. He sounded concerned. *I assumed that you did it to let me in.*

Why were my barriers so weak?

What were you saying about Brace? I decided to worry about it later.

When you were melded people worried less about you. For us, knowing you always had Brace watching out for you was a relief. Now they think you're alone and therefore want to protect you more.

I sighed. *These things certainly have a ricocheting effect.*

It will be further reaching than you ever expected. Now try and reinforce your barriers before the Princeps arrive.

I hadn't had to work on my mental protection for a long time. I pulled on my energy and encased my thoughts.

More, Josian said.

I added another layer and waited. He nodded a couple of times at me. I'd take that. He must not be able to get through and if he couldn't no other Walker – except probably Brace – could either.

"When is the meeting?" I asked out loud.

"I've set everyone up at the large dining table," Lallielle said. "They should be here within the hour."

"Will we be present?" Ria asked. "If you're discussing the Seventine then we should be in there."

Sometimes the Queen was really obvious in Ria's personality.

"Yes," Josian said, "it would be for the best if you were part of the discussions."

Lallielle led us through the house to the formal dining room near the back. We never usually ate there, preferring the more casual atmosphere of the space that bordered the kitchen. But that table wasn't big enough for everyone, so into the overly fancy room we crowded.

"I think I'll wait outside." Ladre's words drew our attention.

I'd forgotten how distinct the lisping tongue of the Spurn's was.

"Talli will fill me in on what was discussed."

Talina ran over to give him a hug. They touched foreheads briefly and he was gone.

"Well, I'm not leaving." Dune said. "I need to know when Fury and I can return to Crais. I'm worried about my dragoona."

I stared at him. "I can take you back there whenever you want, Dune. You don't have to stay with Fury all the time."

He laughed. "You've never been mated, Abby, so it's hard for you to understand, but where Fury goes I go. Especially if there's danger."

I opened my mouth to reply, before slamming it shut again. What was I supposed to say? Everyone here, bar two, thought I was an independent, unmated half-Walker. No one could see the pain inside, the tattered golden embers of the cord in my mind. No one knew.

Lucy gave me a sympathetic smile.

Lallielle interrupted the awkward moment by declaring she had to get refreshments, and then, as she left the room, the rest of us moved into our assigned places. There were ten seats on either side of the table and one on each end. The four of us half-Walkers sat on one side. The other side was for the Princeps. Josian took his seat there. Dune and Lucy sat away from the table in two of those waiting chairs against the wall. When Lallielle returned she had Grantham, Krahn and Nos following her.

We rose to greet them, before sitting down again. Which was a waste, because at that moment Jedi and Tatiana entered the room. Once the formal greetings and small talk were out of the way everyone got down to discussing the situation with the Seventine.

"So there are four released now?" Tatiana spoke. She looked calm and her words were strong. "And there's nothing to be done except collect the rest of the girls and try and figure out how to lock them back in their prison."

"We tried the ritual of the four." I addressed the room. "And it didn't work. Br —" I caught myself before I said his name, but it was close. "We think it was because they were releasing the fourth at the same time we were performing the ritual. The energy collided or something and the Seventine were stronger."

"Which doesn't bode well for future battles?" Grantham said.

Josian nodded. "This is true, and for that reason we've decided the girls need more training, to strengthen their powers."

He looked across the table at the four of us. "We've proposed that each of you spend some time with the Princeps of your clan. They will be responsible for assessing your power and training by any means they can."

I froze. Josian hadn't mentioned that before.

"Do you think it's a good idea that we split up?" It felt wrong. We were a team and splitting us seemed counter-productive to strengthening us. "I feel like we should be working on the strength of our bonds with each other."

"Let's try this first," he said. "Besides, while they're training you'll have time to move on to Nephilius, Dronish and Earth. It's just as important that you find the rest of the girls."

I bit my lip for a moment but didn't question him again. Josian would surely know better than I did what was going to help us.

"My Princeps isn't here," Talina said. "Where's Brace?"

"Sorry I'm late. I wasn't sure if I could escape Abernath, but my schedule ended up clearing."

My heart stopped.

I mean literally stopped beating in my chest.

He was standing in the doorway, filling it with his giant height and breadth. His warm smile took in everyone, myself included, but where he would have normally moved toward me, or given me an extra look, he just continued past.

Lucy and Josian were both staring at me with twin expressions of concern. I swallowed and shoved the pain down again, which allowed my heart to beat again. I could do this; he was going to be around a lot. Ripping off a bandage.

"So fill me in on what I missed?" He pulled out a chair, which was thankfully not across from mine.

"Just that each of the girls will be going with their Princeps for some intense one-on-one training. And that Aribella will continue on to gather the next half-Walker," Grantham answered.

"And which is the next planet?" He turned to me, his brown eyes twinkling.

"Uh." I cleared my throat. "Nephilius." I had to clear my throat again. "Will you excuse me?"

I pushed my chair back and, before anyone could ask why, dashed from the room. I made it to the hallway washroom before I lost it. My chest heaved as the sobs burst from me. I gripped the edge of the sink, fighting against the grief, trying my best to contain the agony pouring from my soul. I hadn't cried before then. It was as if I'd been numb from the moment I woke. But seeing him, hearing his voice with none of its usual love and warmth, had reiterated how truly alone I was. Ripping off a bandage – I was a fool and Lucy was right – it was more like ripping off an appendage. My heart.

Arms encircled me from behind. Lucy held me and I held the sink. We stood there until I was strong enough to let go.

"Everyone's leaving, Abbs. They were going to wait for you, but I told them you had a bad headache and probably went to lie down."

I laughed. "And the first half of that is not even a lie, Luce."

The mirror reflected back my red-eyed splotchy self, but as I stood there watching I could see my skin clearing. The red disappeared and then the physical evidence of my pain was gone.

"Do my marks look less intense?" I asked Lucy.

She examined me in the reflective surface. "I don't know, maybe a little less shine."

What could that mean?

I splashed my face a few times, and rubbed my temples to relieve the pounding there. I didn't even know Walkers got headaches. Lucy opened the door for us to leave and there was Brace against the wall. Propped up with one foot back against it.

"Do you have to stand there all sexy like?" Lucy demanded. "What do you want, Brace?"

I put a hand on her arm. She was overreacting. He would have no idea why she was upset.

He straightened. His dark hair fell across his beautiful face.

"I just wanted to make sure you were okay?" He looked straight into my eyes and I knew there was still a connection between us.

Even without his memories Brace was drawn to me and he would have no idea why.

"You ran out so fast. Was it something I said?" he joked to lighten the mood.

I smiled the brightest one I could manage. "Just a headache. I think I've been world-jumping a bit too frequently. Thanks for your concern." I sidled past him, Lucy running interference between us so we wouldn't touch.

"See you later, Brace," I called over my shoulder.

He looked solemn standing there, confusion on his features. But he was distracted as Talina emerged with Ladre. I knew they'd be heading to Abernath with him. To my home. I fought hard to stop the tears.

"Aribella."

I spun at the deep voice that called from the white room.

"Josian said you needed to talk with me."

It was Jedi. He looked less exotic without his white marks but still exceptionally handsome. I nodded a few times, excited that someone was forcing me to focus on my mission and not my love life. Lucy left me with him. She said she had to go speak with Josian; update him on how I was doing.

I stepped into the room. "You told me to find you when I asked why. So what I want to know is why are they releasing them now? Do you know?"

He took a seat on the long white couch, indicating I should sit next to him. I hesitated, finally dropping down with lots of space between us. I missed having the barrier of a mate between me and other men. I wasn't so vain that I thought many men were going to come beating down my door, but it was still an annoyance.

"I haven't said anything because this is simply me piecing together lots of information over the last thousand years." His gaze was focused as he started to talk. "Allegedly in the beginning when this star-system was formed, the collision of power created the seven originals, the Seventine and First World. Then slowly over time the other planets

330

were formed from the energy of First World. We are coming up to the anniversary of this moment. When the clock clicks over on a billion years all seven worlds will align, along with all of their tethers. We call this the convergence."

I was starting to comprehend what he was saying, and I could feel my face tightening as the horror spread through me.

"So when they all align, that will allow the Seventine to just –?"

"Sever every tether in one swift move."

He finished the sentence for me.

"What's the date of this convergence?" I choked out.

He shook his head. "The exact date is information lost to history. But I've been doing some advanced calculations. I hope to be able to narrow it down to a manageable time period. I'm getting close but just not there yet."

I nodded. "Let me know as soon as you have any idea of the time frame."

He reached out and rested a hand on my clenched fists and white knuckles. "Don't worry so. They can't sever the ultimate tether without all seven of their power."

I smiled before gently removing my hands from under his. I stood then.

"Thank you, Jedi, for this information. I'll hear from you when you've done your calculations?"

He stood also. "I'll be in touch. Stay safe." He strode from the room.

As soon as he was gone I sprinted back to the dining area. I had to find Josian; he needed to hear this development.

"So you're telling me that if we don't stop or re-imprison the Seventine before this date of convergence they could destroy everything in one sever?" Lucy let her shock creep into that question.

I nodded. "Yes, Jedi thinks that might be the case."

Josian sighed. "Let's not worry about this yet. It doesn't change our mission for now. We need to discuss the next planet. Are you ready to leave immediately?"

I felt a little off center, but really that was to be expected after losing my other half, so I nodded. "Yes, I'm fine to leave straight away. Better to find the half-Walkers soon. We know the Seventine will be off severing tethers and gathering energy to release the fifth."

"Well, Grantham did some scouting on Nephilius for you."

The man himself stepped into the room. His warm cat-like eyes rested on me.

"Aribella," he boomed in his friendly tones. "I popped over to the planet last week, just to see what you're up against. And I think there's only one way you're going to be able to find the half-Walker."

He paused. I raised my brows at him.

"You're going to have to fight in the tournament."

I laughed. "What do you mean?"

He laughed with me. "You should love this, Aribella. Nephilius is a warrior planet. They value courage, bravery and the ability to kick ass. Every year they hold a massive tournament where they have fight rounds. If you lose you're eliminated, otherwise you advance to the next round."

I straightened. I could use some good fighting to get my mind off Brace, but I hadn't trained in months. My skills were a little rusty.

"The competition starts in a month. I've entered your name. So now we're going to have to train you up, because you can't use any obvious energy power, only fight skills."

I looked around the room.

"Well, looks like it's time to get training."

Chapter 18

Brace

She was the most stunning woman he had ever seen. Brace had met Aribella, daughter of Josian, before, of course, but it felt as if her presence kicked him in the gut this time. Followed by a sharp jab to the chest.

He had only sat across from her for a few moments, but as those stunning green eyes looked anywhere but at him he felt the need to capture her attention. But before he had an opportunity she had run from the room.

His instincts urged him to follow, make sure she was okay. He'd tried to reason with himself; he had important things to do. Abernath was a mess and he didn't have time for Aribella.

And yet he'd been unable to stop himself from checking that she was alright. He was still standing in the hallway. The light, flowery scent that was distinctly hers lingered around him. He shook his head as a strange fragment of an image crossed his mind. Aribella was naked in bed, her head thrown back as she laughed in uncontrollable gasps. Her mass of curls falling everywhere.

And then it was gone.

Brace reached up and rubbed at his temples. Was that some type of fantasy spasm, because he knew he would remember if he'd ever had her naked in bed before.

The door opened and there she was before him. Her tiny blond friend, Lucy, was clutching one of her hands. His eyes briefly dropped to Lucy but she held no interest for him. He preferred them less fragile and she was Colton's, anyways.

Lucy's features hardened as she leaned toward him. "Do you have to stand there all sexy like?" she demanded. "What do you want, Brace."

He straightened, pushing back his hair and wondering where this animosity had come from. Probably something to do with Colton.

"I just wanted to make sure you were okay?"

He looked directly into Aribella's eyes. He could feel the connection. His hands itched to reach out and trace the contours of her beautiful face, touch that ivory skin that looked soft and perfect. Why did he feel as if he'd touched her a million times before? To stop himself from reaching for her he tried to lighten the mood.

"You ran out so fast. Was it something I said?"

She smiled fully for the first time and Brace almost scooped her up and ran from the room. If he had to tie her up until she admitted to this insane energy and connection between them … well, it was starting to seem like a viable option.

"Just a headache. I think I've been world-jumping a bit too frequently. Thanks for your concern."

He tried to remember what question she was answering. He was acting like a love-sick fool and at five hundred years he was just too old for that.

She slid past him. He clenched his fists to stop from reaching out to her.

"See you later, Brace," she called over her shoulder.

"You can count on it, Aribella." He said quietly as she disappeared.

A week later he was sparring with Colton in the Abernath training hall. He was happy that his words were starting to have some effect. Only half the men were there that day.

"What's up with you? Your efforts are even more half-assed than usual." His friend was watching him a half-smirk on his face.

Brace pulled himself up from the mat. Usually he could wipe the floor with Colton, but today his focus was off.

"Woman troubles."

Colton's smirk increased. Brace's last relationship had been fifty years before, now he preferred an uncomplicated life. And he held out the hope he would eventually find his mate. And while Brace was happy that Colton had found his other half in Lucy, he wanted to find the same, the one to quell the endless loneliness inside him.

Brace threw out his legs and, taking Colton by surprise, hooked behind his friend's knee. Colton landed on his ass.

"You can talk, Colt, if I have to hear one more time how sexy Lucy is."

Colton's eyes hardened. "I've never said that. Lucy deserves better than to be talked about like she's just a hot chick down the street."

Brace let a grin cross his face as Colton hung his head, swearing.

"I told you, old friend," Brace said, getting to his feet. "She's the first female where you've cared more for her than yourself. Definitely glad you've found your mate."

"My damn wolf is driving me crazy. He demands that we get our asses to First World and find our mate," Colton snarled. "But Lucy said she's got something going on with Abby."

Brace laughed. "Those two are an interesting pair. And try not to smother your mate, Colt. I know it goes against Walker and wolf instincts, but it's better to have an equal relationship."

Colton shot out a jab, which Brace sidestepped. His follow-around elbow cracked Colton in the jaw.

"You're the most over-protective male on Abernath," Colton said. "How can you judge me for the same thing?"

Brace shook his head. "There're differences between being protective and smothering every facet of personality from a woman. Why fall in love with all that strength and then try to squash it out of her because you're afraid to lose her?"

It took no effort to knock the distracted Colton onto his ass again. Brace stood over him, hands on his hips.

"You're a good man. And you will be for Lucy."

Colton nodded. "I'm not sure you're right but only time will tell. And I know I can't stay away from her. I have a constant need to be where she is."

Brace stopped. "Well, I have to go back to see Josian soon. You can have some Lucy time ... and I feel that I should be spending some time with Aribella."

Colton eyed him, his expression curious.

"It's all because of Abby, isn't it? The reason you're so distracted and crazy at the moment."

Brace wasn't going to lie to his friend anymore. "Yes. I can't stop thinking about her. And the dreams every night ... I don't know what the hell's going on."

"Dreams?" Colton asked.

"Yep, dreams as if we've been together before. Just snippets of a life that I wished to have with a mate."

Colton bounced across the floor toward the door. "Sounds like something worth exploring."

Brace laughed as he followed at a slower pace. But Colton was right; it was time to see if there was something there.

He was going to find Aribella. And she better prepare, because when Brace set his mind to something, nothing changed it, and right now the stunning redhead was set firmly in his sights.

***

Please, if you loved this book, could you do me a huge favor and post a review on Amazon and/or Goodreads. Reviews are so valuable to independent authors and I'd appreciate your feedback. – Jaymin ☺

http://www.facebook.com/pages/Jaymin-Eve/519939168016600

Or email jaymineve@gmail.com

About the Author

Jaymin Eve is a twenty-nine-year-old with the best job in the world. When she's not being a mother to two beautiful girls, you'll find her hammering away at her computer lost in her fantasy worlds, or traveling to far-off places for family fun and exploration.

She'd love to hear from you, so find her at
http://www.facebook.com/pages/Jaymin-Eve/519939168016600

Or email jaymineve@gmail.com

28993893R00194

Made in the USA
San Bernardino, CA
11 January 2016